A PERFECT MARRIAGE

Sally Lachlan has a secret. A chance meeting with the charismatic geneticist Anthony Blake reawakens her desire for love. But as Sally finally lets down her guard, daughter Charlie begins to ask questions about her father and what really happened all those years ago. Both the past and the future are places Sally prefers not to think about, but if she wants to find happiness, she must first come to terms with her previous marriage. Only then can she be honest with Charlie . . . and herself. Set in THEN and NOW, *A Perfect Marriage* is a traumatic and harrowing look at love and loss, forgiveness and hope; of a daughter's enduring love for her mother, and a mother's quest for peace of mind.

ALISON BOOTH

A
PERFECT
MARRIAGE

Complete and Unabridged

AURORA
Leicester

First published in Great Britain in 2018 by
RedDoor Publishing Ltd

First Aurora Edition
published 2019
by arrangement with
RedDoor Publishing Ltd

Excerpt on page ix reproduced with permission
of The Provost and Scholars of King's College,
Cambridge and The Society of Authors as the
E.M. Forster Estate

A catalogue record for this book is available
from the British Library.

ISBN 978-1-78782-082-1

Published by
F. A. Thorpe (Publishing)
Anstey, Leicestershire

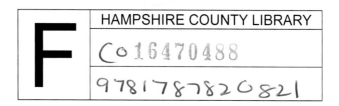

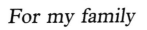

For my family

'There is much good luck in the world, but it is luck. We are none of us safe. We are children, playing or quarrelling on the line'

E.M. Forster, The Longest Journey (1907)

1

THEN

The body lay on a gurney in the middle of the room. When the coroner's assistant uncovered the head, my heart began to knock against my ribcage and I could feel the thump-thump-thump of a migraine starting.

The assistant stood back and I stepped forward.

The body was his all right. They must have cleaned him up. I put out a hand to touch the pale forehead. It was icy cold from the refrigeration. There were fine lines around his eyes and his blond hair was tousled. He was beautiful still, in spite of what had happened to him.

I waited as the minutes passed by, almost expecting to see his chest rise and fall, almost expecting to see the eyelids flutter open. I forgot about the coroner's assistant until she gave a discreet cough. Turning away from the body, I nodded to her. As I walked past, she took a step towards me and lightly patted my forearm.

Outside, sadness and relief wavered through my head like paper kites tossed about in a high wind. I bought a copy of the *Evening Standard* from the newsvendor on the corner. On the front page there was yet another picture of that woman. Behind the piles of newspapers was a wire rack with yesterday's headlines that I knew I'd never forget.

A blast of diesel fumes from a passing bus precipitated my migraine. I leaned against the mottled trunk of a plane tree. When the nausea came, I stood at the edge of the pavement and threw up in the gutter. No one appeared to notice, certainly no one stopped.

I carried on retching until my stomach hurt. After a while, a smartly dressed woman asked if I needed help. Her kindness made me weep, hot silent tears. 'Is there someone I can call?' she said, her arm around my shoulders.

I hiccoughed a couple of times and accepted the tissues she was holding out. 'I'm fine, thanks,' I said, after wiping my eyes.

And I was. That part of my life was well and truly behind me now. I could do with a drop of water though. My mouth felt parched and I could barely swallow. But before I could get on with my life there was the coroner to deal with. She was waiting for me on the steps to the mortuary building.

All I wanted was some peace for Charlie and me. But there was no guarantee that would come easily.

2

NOW

I see the young man's back first, as he squeezes past the passengers cramming their luggage into the overhead lockers. His fair hair curls over the collar of his cream trench coat. He is so tall he has to stoop slightly as he presses past. Now he is looking at the seat numbers on the other side of the aisle. Although people are sitting there, perhaps he thinks they are not in their rightful places: the only unoccupied seat in this part of the plane is next to me. I pick up the book and newspaper I had placed on the empty seat.

The man turns and I realise my mistake. He is not young at all; he must be in his late thirties or maybe older. His hair is not fair either, but light brown finely streaked with white, as if he's had highlights from some expensive Bond Street hair salon.

He mumbles a greeting. I nod, hoping this won't be interpreted as an invitation to begin a conversation. After handing his carry-on luggage to a flight attendant to stow at the back of the plane, he sits down with a sigh. I engross myself in my book, reading the same paragraph twice without taking in any of it. Then I steal a sideways look at my companion at the same time that he is sneaking a look at me. He smiles disarmingly. I smile back but don't put down my novel.

The plane begins to taxi along the runway and in a few moments we are airborne. Below is the shimmering snake of the River Thames, and row after row of houses, an ever-expanding vista. One of those is mine, my little terrace in Kentish Town. Soon we are swooping into a thick white bank of cloud, and upwards into a blazing blue, and London has gone.

I try to read but again I'm not taking it in. The man next to me has extracted something from his briefcase, a hardback book. Without turning my head, I glance at its cover but can't make out the title. He turns it so I can read the dust jacket, and we both laugh. It's the new novel by Peter Carey.

We have left England far behind and are flying over water. The sea, solid like a piece of frosted glazing, is patterned with fine ripples. A few ships are dotted in the distance, like flies squashed on the glass. The sun glints off the surface, glittering and gold-rimmed.

'Would you like lunch, Madame?' The flight attendant holds out a tray as if she is offering rations to a particularly ill-favoured animal in a zoo.

I decline. I ate at the airport and am not hungry. But the man next to me whispers, 'I'll have it if you don't want it. I'm starving.'

At once I tell the flight attendant that I have changed my mind and she passes me the tray. My neighbour thanks me profusely and makes a start on his lunch. As he opens his water cup, he says, 'You're not a biologist, are you? I know there are a few on this flight.' He has a pleasant voice; more resonant than deep, it seems to vibrate from the centre of his chest.

I nod and offer him my quiche. He transfers it onto his tray. 'So you're going to the same conference as me,' he says. 'I haven't seen you on the conference circuit.'

'I haven't been to many international ones. This is only my second.'

'I travel quite a lot. Too much really but it's part of the job. Why so few conferences for you?'

'I'm a single mother.' I watch for his reaction. I've grown to enjoy the male retreat on learning this information. It's a way of preserving my independence and my cynicism.

'That must be hard.' His tone is matter-of-fact. The piece of information I've given him means nothing to him.

He takes a large mouthful of quiche. He eats quickly, as do people who are used to institutional food. Probably he was educated at a boarding school, a posh one at that. For a moment I consider telling him about my daughter Charlie, but think better of it. When he has finished he puts down his knife and fork; he smiles and asks about my children.

Only one child, I tell him and soon find myself explaining how hard it is to get away to conferences, although my daughter is a dream and has never caused me any trouble, at least not yet. He seems interested, so I tell him that she's seventeen and doing her A-levels.

'You look too young to have a teenage daughter,' he says. This is the usual response, the conventional response. He is being gallant, as

5

they always are. But today I am pleased. It's as if I gave away my scepticism with my quiche, barely five minutes ago. I explain that I had my daughter when I was twenty. I don't want him to think I'm older than I am.

'You look much younger than thirty-seven,' he says.

'I see you're good at sums.' I pass him the tired-looking chocolate mousse from my lunch tray. Probably I've been talking too much; I resolve not to say any more about Charlie.

While he polishes off his second dessert, I speculate on his family background. He will have a charming professional wife — a lawyer perhaps — and two beautiful children, whose digital pictures he might show me later in the flight, when he opens the laptop that is almost certainly concealed in his briefcase. 'What about you?' I ask.

'No kids, I'm afraid, and I'm not married either.' He doesn't look at me but tidies the various pieces of packaging on his tray, eventually returning them to a semblance of order. He might always be methodical or perhaps my question has unsettled him. I feel embarrassed, as if I've been prying. It's my fault we are on this topic; I shouldn't have gone on at such length about my daughter. But then I remember that he asked me first. He looks at me and grins; the awkward moment passes and is replaced by a feeling almost of ease.

The flight attendant comes by with coffee. She fills my cup first but avoids my eye. She lingers over pouring my neighbour's coffee and offers him an additional mousse; she has several spare in the galley. After he declines, we grapple in silence with the aluminium foil covers on our pots of milk. Mine comes off with a rush; the milk spatters all over my hand and drips onto the tray. My neighbour passes me his napkin and asks me my name.

'Sally Lachlan,' he repeats after I've told him. I like the way he pronounces the syllables, on different notes. 'You're at University College, aren't you? I read one of your papers in the latest issue of *Trends in Genetics*.'

I am delighted. I saw somewhere that on average two people in the world read each academic journal article: it's gratifying to meet one of them. 'Was that the one on stem cells?' I ask.

'What, do you have more than one paper in that issue?' He is laughing now.

'Was it on stem cells from skin?'

'From skin and not human embryos — isn't that what you work on? That will have ethical implications, won't it?'

'You mean there won't be any?'

'Do you ever answer questions, Sally, as well as ask them?'

'Sometimes,' I say, laughing. 'What's your name?'

'Anthony Blake.'

My laughter dries up. I hadn't imagined Anthony Blake would be close to my age. He has been publishing for so long I'd assumed he'd be nearing retirement. He has been at Imperial College for a number of years, so it's surprising that we haven't met before, although I know he visits the United States frequently.

The flight attendant takes away our trays as we approach the Spanish coast. The plane is dropping, wheeling like a bird of prey over cracked brown hills. The landing gear descends and the plane floats down towards the runway. As the wheels touch the tarmac, I look at my companion at the same moment that he turns towards me. For the first time I see his face full frontal. He smiles and I feel a shock of recognition. I smile back. His eyes are a deep blue.

The moment is broken by the hubbub of excited voices, the click of seat belts unfastening, the opening of the overhead lockers. Someone is calling, 'Sally! Sally!' and I look up to see a colleague waving for me to join her. I turn to Anthony, who offers me his hand, a strange gesture.

'It's been really good to meet you,' he says. I shake his hand, somewhat awkwardly in the confined space. It is cool and dry and I don't want to let go of it. Next he collects his coat and briefcase, and is given his luggage by the simpering flight attendant. After extricating myself more slowly, I leave the plane with my colleague.

At the luggage carousel, I notice Anthony on the far side, standing with a man I haven't seen before, probably also a conference delegate. I watch Anthony watching me. I am at the mercy of my biochemistry now. Isn't this what attraction is? I can almost feel the neurotransmitters making connections. Watch out, body: here come the monoamines. Watch out, body: dopamine, adrenaline, and serotonin are on the loose.

3

NOW

My hotel bedroom is huge, with heavy dark wooden furniture that is dwarfed by the expanse of red quarry-tiled floor. It is past sunset and the shutters have already been fastened. I open the French windows and unlock the shutters. There is an almost full moon hanging in a navy-blue sky. The moon illuminates a narrow lawn below, edged on the far side by a paved walk that follows the curve of the battlements defining the edge of this rocky headland. Beyond the ramparts, the Atlantic Ocean glimmers; waves are crashing against the rocks below the stone castle walls. I stand there for a few minutes, breathing deeply the fresh salty air. This harbour is the spot from which, over half a millennium ago, Christopher Columbus set sail to find North America.

Yesterday I might have found that thought sobering. Tonight I find it exciting. I fold the shutters back again but leave one window open to air the room.

The bathroom is enormous; like a mausoleum, its walls and floor are lined with white marble. I turn on the lights and survey myself in the mirror. The spotlighting illuminates the auburn hair of this pale stranger, this woman whom I have met today for the first time in a plane on the way to Vigo. Perhaps Anthony Blake is also looking at himself in a mirror in a bathroom that is the pair of mine, somewhere in this lavish hotel, and thinking of me. In this light my eyes look a darker brown than usual, and the freckles on my nose stand out harshly against my white skin. I dab my nose with powder and brush some highlighter onto my cheekbones. I cannot find a comb, so run fingers through my springy hair until it stands up around my face like the padded coiffure of an Edwardian lady. I smile at my reflection and try to imagine what a stranger would see. A quite pretty woman, a quite ordinary woman, I can't decide which. But how silly I'm being and now it's almost nine o'clock. I collect my jacket.

In the queue leading into the dining room I join some colleagues. We are at the end of the line, and cannot choose where to sit; there are only a few seats left at a table on the far side of the room next to the windows.

After a few minutes I see Anthony moving towards us. 'May I join you?' he asks. He is not expressing any preference. There is no alternative: these are the only vacant seats.

'Of course,' several of us say in unison.

Anthony sits down opposite me. Again I experience a feeling of recognition. He reminds me of someone but I can't think who. Perhaps if I talk to him I shall remember.

'Sally,' a Swedish man says, 'you never told me what happened to the organoids your lab grew from human skin cells.'

I tell him about our organoids, those tiny

organ buds that could be so useful to regenerative medicine. While I talk, I am crumbling bread in my fingers and looking at Anthony; at the line of his jaw, at the way his hair sits against his collar.

'They did that at Stockholm too,' the man says.

Now I am watching Anthony's hands as he twists his water glass; they are strong with long, slightly blunt-ended fingers. When he smiles at me, my skin starts to feel different. Like that moment on a hot summer's night when you step into warm water and there is no difference in temperature between your body and its surrounds, and the water glides over your skin like silk. Blind-sided for an instant by longing, or perhaps it is nostalgia for past summer holidays and the safety of childhood, I lose concentration and am brought into the present only when the Swedish man asks me a question.

Once dinner is over, people at our table drift off, some to the bar, some to their rooms to prepare their talks or to read the papers that have been distributed. Anthony and I are left behind, facing each other across the table.

He smiles. His face creases up but it creases in the right spots. He has a kind face. A serendipitous quirk of nature perhaps, for who knows what he is really like. While we talk more about the organoids and the problems of their short life, my biochemistry shifts into overdrive and myriad neurotransmitters signal a story that is far more distracting than the organoids. Anthony's gaze never leaves mine; it is impossible to look away. I am being pulled towards him, I feel as if I could dive into the pools of his dark blue eyes.

We are interrupted by a small entourage led by a man in a suit, and it's clear that it's not me they wish to talk to. Although Anthony introduces me, I make my excuses. I don't want to appear to be hanging around him, like a groupie around a rock star, and anyway I am nervous about my talk tomorrow. I need to read through my paper at least one more time. Only Anthony notices that I am going. 'Goodnight, Sally,' he says.

No wonder he is universally liked.

★ ★ ★

Someone has been in my room while we've been at dinner. The window has been closed again and the cover removed from the vast bed. This intervention, the custom at many hotels, comes as a shock. I feel irrationally annoyed, as if my house has been broken into. On one side of the bed — not the side that I would have chosen — the sheet has been folded over to form a triangle, inviting me to sleep. I fold back the other corner of the sheet and open the window before picking up the phone and calling my home number.

'Hello?' Charlie sounds breathless. How lovely it is to hear her voice even though it's barely half a day since I left home.

'Hi, darling.' I picture her in her dressing gown, standing dripping by the phone. I have a knack of calling her when she is in the bath.

12

'I'm not in the bath.' Charlie is laughing; she can often read my mind. 'We've just come in from seeing a film. How was your trip?' Her school friend, Amrita, is staying with her in my absence. Practising for going to university, Charlie calls it. Presumably this means drinking and maybe smoking, but you have to let go at some stage. This is the first time I have left Charlie at home for more than a day or so but I'm not really worried. Both of them are more mature than some of my colleagues and Amrita's parents live only a street away.

I tell Charlie about my day but I don't mention Anthony.

'Anyone worth talking to?' she says.

'No, not really.'

'A long way to go for nothing.'

'The interesting part comes tomorrow.'

'That's when you give your talk,' she says, laughing. 'By the way, I got a letter today, from Marge in Australia. She said she found some old photos and things that I might like to have.'

My hand clutching the phone becomes clammy and I grunt a response.

'She stuck them in a cupboard after Grandpa died and forgot all about them. I'm so thrilled, Mum.'

'Is Marge going to send them to you?' My heart is thumping too hard. I walk the few paces to the window and inhale deeply, feeling the cool air fill my lungs. For years I've known that at some stage I'll have to tell Charlie the truth. And for year after year I've procrastinated.

'I've written to her saying I'd love to have

13

them. You'll be interested too, Mum.'

'Very.'

When we've finished talking, I shut the window, fighting against the wind that has risen. Old photos and *things*: I don't like the sound of that. I open a small bottle of Scotch from the minibar and take two sips. For medicinal purposes, that's what Charlie's grandfather used to say.

The window frames and shutters are rattling in a syncopated rhythm as the gale howls around the hotel, trying to find a way in. The waves are crashing against the rocks no more than thirty metres away from where I'm sitting, on the raft of my double bed on the edge of the ocean.

I finish the Scotch and follow it up with a glass of still water. My muscles relax as the alcohol takes over. Slipping between sheets that feel cool and slightly damp, I put my arm around the spare pillow, a substitute for the lover I'd like to have, and pull the covers up over us both. It's been years since I've wanted the comfort of a man in my bed. It's not just any man I'm thinking of, it's the one with the beautiful hands; the one who sat opposite me at dinner.

The man I barely know.

I slip abruptly into sleep.

★   ★   ★

We are in Cornwall visiting my parents, who have a house on the south coast. They have hired a large rowing boat to take us out into the bay. Perhaps we shall reach the small rocky island not far from the shore and picnic there. My father pushes the boat off from the stone quay. He and Jeff are rowing; they are perched side by side in the middle of the boat, and pull us effortlessly into the deeper water. My mother and I are sitting in the stern. Charlie, kneeling on the narrow seat in the bow, is watching the boat cutting through the smooth satin of the sea. Next to her is a small pile of books.

It's one of those rare summer days when the light is so alive that the air seems to be throbbing. Glancing back at the village, I spot my parents' cottage, white-washed like all the other houses lining the harbour, and marked out by the profusion of blue and white flowers spilling over the low front wall; my mother is never garish with her choice of plants. The low hill behind the town has been burned a golden yellow by the unusually hot summer.

When I turn seawards again, the water has changed. There are huge waves rolling in, even though we are still ten metres or so from the end of the wall that shelters this little harbour. The sky to the south-west is covered with low black clouds and a curtain of rain is advancing rapidly towards us.

'We should go back,' I tell my mother.

She smiles placidly at me. 'You always were a worrier. Your father will look after us.' And she turns her gaze back towards the island as we plough over the waves, moving erratically from peak to trough.

'Let's go back!' I shout to my father and Jeff. My voice is caught up by the wind that has risen, and is thrown back at me.

My father and Jeff say nothing; they grin tolerantly at me as if to humour me, or perhaps to save their breath for the effort of rowing. They have their backs to the swell, and are continuing to pull at their oars as if there is nothing wrong. Leaning forward, I grab Jeff's knee and point behind him. But he laughs and carries on rowing in complete harmony with my father.

Once beyond the rocks, piled up to shelter the harbour entrance, we are caught up in a raging, boiling sea that tosses our boat about, as if it's an insignificant piece of driftwood. Jeff and my father are forced to stop rowing and the boat spins dangerously around, full circle, so that we are still pointing out to sea. My mother and I are hanging on grimly to the gunwale and Charlie is crouching in the bow.

'Turn around!'

'Go back!'

Jeff and my father are yelling at each other, while simultaneously grabbing at the oars that have been wrenched out of their hands by the force of the water. My father's oar is still in the rowlock, but Jeff's has slipped out and he reaches it only just in time to prevent it from vanishing into the waves. By some miracle they manage to turn the boat about and we are catapulted back into the relative calm of the harbour. The bottom of the dinghy is filled with water and I find Charlie's sodden books at my feet. I pick them up and fan through the pages.

'I've got your books, Charlie!' I shout through the gap between the two rowers. It's starting to rain and I tuck the books under my shirt.

'Charlie!' I call again.

And at that moment I realise that Charlie has gone.

Rain is streaming down my face and it's hard to see clearly. We cannot spot Charlie anywhere.

'Charlie!'

'Charlie!'

We are all screaming now.

And then I wake up shouting and my face is streaming with tears.

4

NOW

I wrench myself fully awake and stagger across the room to where the light switch should be. My skin feels cold and damp and there is panic rising like bile in my throat. My heart is racing; my feet are poised for flight as I grope my way along the wall. But there is no way out, no escape from this feeling of loss.

I wipe my eyes with the sleeve of my nightshirt. My vision clears and I see a glimmer of light: green digits on a radio clock that show 01:20 hours. Here I am, not in Kentish Town but in my hotel bedroom on the Spanish edge of the Atlantic. And I can't have slept for much more than an hour.

I put on my suit jacket and unfasten the windowpanes and shutters, to let the wind blow into the room. Kneeling on the floor, I breathe deeply until my fear has gone; as it always does once I'm fully awake. For a moment I wonder if I should phone Charlie. But no, she is fine, this is an irrational fear. Charlie will worry that I am worrying about her, instead of having the good time that I want her to have while I am away.

The moon is no longer visible and, as I watch, the last of the stars are obliterated by a swift-moving bank of clouds rolling in from the west, just like in my dream. For years these dreams of loss have plagued me; loss of my family or my friends, or even of inanimate but important objects like keys — valuable objects that will keep the forces of nature at bay.

While I'm kneeling, the wind drops. The background roaring of the waves appears to grow to a crescendo, until suddenly the drumming of rain drowns this out. As the clouds release their burden, I lean over the sill and hold my face up to the downpour, until my dream is washed away and the water starts to dampen my jacket.

But I stay here by the window, looking out at the wet night.

I think of Jeff and me adrift on the Atlantic Ocean on our way to La Spezia, on our honeymoon all those years ago. We must have passed right by this stretch of Spanish coast.

But Jeff is dead. For nearly ten years Jeff has been dead. It is still hard sometimes to comprehend this. The man I once loved so much is now a pile of bones under the ground in a cemetery in Somerset. Yet he lives on so vividly in my life. And in my actions.

I think of Anthony again but it's no longer a pleasant fantasy of what might happen between us. Instead, my stomach contracts into a tight knot, and a black wave of apprehension washes over my body. I fill my lungs with air and the anxiety eases, but I stay there peering out at the rain, until the dampness starts to soak through my suit jacket and I remember that I have to wear it again tomorrow.

Back in bed I'm feeling wideawake. I log into my laptop and open my talk for tomorrow afternoon — this afternoon now: *Dishing up mini-organs: How to grow pluripotent stem cells in the laboratory.* I begin to read. Work is soothing; work is a panacea. After an hour or so I'm ready to try sleeping again. The rain has stopped and the waves are a distant regular pounding. Adrift, afloat, I am on a calm sea again.

★   ★   ★

I wake up late and dress hurriedly. Breakfast is over and the conference has begun by the time I pick up a coffee from the machine in the foyer. There are only a few empty seats in the auditorium, all at the back. No one I know is sitting here. My colleagues are further forward; punctual people who remember to set their alarm clocks. Only after I locate Anthony sitting in a middle row do I realise I've been looking for him. The coffee is reviving and I begin to feel like a member of the human race again.

The morning flashes by. One by one the presenters stand up in front of this audience of genetics and biomedical experts; one by one they give their spiel, show their visual aids, receive their questions, defend their ideas; and one by one they return again to form the audience for the next presentation. In spite of the variety of languages that the participants speak in their own countries, the academic language and customs are the same the world over.

Anthony gives his lecture immediately before lunch. He briefly mentions the work of his team on cloning, but his purpose here, he tells us, is to provide an overview on the subject. His talk is well structured, his logic is flawless; but there is nothing dry about his presentation, for he speaks with great passion, gesturing as he talks with those beautiful hands. At the end, a man with a strong Greek accent raises the inevitable question of human cloning for treating infertile couples. Anthony explains about the enormous failure rate in cloning, and that even when an animal has been successfully cloned, its DNA usually contains abnormalities. Anyway, he says, we all know that developments in transforming mature skin cells into stem cells will remove any medical need to clone embryos.

'That is what I am working on,' says the Greek man. It becomes apparent that the reason he asked a question was to allow him to put forward his own research; he expands on this for several minutes until he is halted by the chair of the session.

'Not before time,' whispers the North American woman sitting next to me. 'That guy always uses question time to push his own work.'

Over lunch the suppressed comments of fifty academics are no longer held back, but erupt from fifty mouths in a deafening roar of conversation. Adrenaline is pumping, ideas are flying — new ones and old ones, original ones and plagiarised ones. There is gossip too, real and invented, about people here, people absent, people known and unknown. All the time I am conscious of Anthony. I swivel around so that I am aware of his position, able to plot his co-ordinates, observing him while not observing him. And I am conscious too that he is aware of me. He never has his back to me. Whoever joins his group or mine is manoeuvred into place so that even with the ebb and flow of people, his face is always turned towards me.

Talks, more talks, and then a half-hour tea break. It is my turn next, but first I must collect my notes and USB stick from my bedroom. As I cross the hotel lobby, a tall figure swings through the door from the outside and stops. Anthony, wearing running shoes, an old T-shirt and shorts, stands dripping in front of me. A bead of sweat makes its way slowly down one cheek; slowly, so slowly, caressing his skin. And I realise that I have raised my hand, and that it's only a few centimetres from his face, that it might touch it and scoop up the little droplet of water. Quickly I pull myself together and push my hair back from my forehead with my raised hand as if this was my original intention. All the while he is talking to me and I have been responding, but I don't know what we have been saying. I am conscious only of my hand and his face.

During my talk, I avoid looking directly at Anthony, but I am aware of his presence. Aware that he's leaning forward slightly, that he's listening intently. The paper is going well, people are laughing — and in the right places too; this must be one of my best presentations. When it is over and the questions begin, I look at Anthony and see that he is smiling at me. He catches my eye and nods his head, the briefest of movements. I look around: am I the only one who has seen this connection?

★ ★ ★

The noise in the room where the reception is being held is loud and it's escalating. I take a glass of wine from the table of drinks and stand at the edge of the crowd, watching. Everyone is talking at once. There are little threads of conversation connecting people. Someone says something that is imperfectly heard; someone else throws back a few words that are loosely related, or perhaps not related at all. And so it goes on: Chinese whispers of conversations, threads of conversations becoming hopelessly entangled. Soon people are speaking even more loudly. Because they can't hear what others tell them, they shout what they have to say, so the level of sound ratchets up, until no one can hear. No one is listening and everyone is speaking, everyone but me. I am out of it. I cannot see how to join in any of these conversations.

At a light touch on my elbow, I look around. 'Nice talk you gave,' Anthony says. 'It's a bit noisy in here, isn't it? Shall we take a stroll around outside?'

We weave our way through the crush towards the French doors; past chunky sweaters, svelte cashmere tops, tailored jackets. No one notices as we brush past. People ordinarily prone to avoid contact are oblivious of our touch. At last we reach the deserted terrace. There is something about Anthony on his own that makes me feel as though we've known each other a long time, as though I won't be judged and found wanting if there are gaps in the conversation.

23

And there are no gaps. My words spill out spontaneously and join his; they hang in the air and vibrate. We warm to our theme; our threads of conversation being woven into a coloured tapestry, an almost tangible connection between us.

As the sun begins to sink below the rim of the ocean, we lean on the parapet and look out to sea. The wind blows up a fine mist that caresses my skin and tastes salty on my lips.

'I'm flying back to London tonight,' Anthony says.

I look away quickly so that he can't see my surprise and disappointment.

'My taxi will be here soon. I thought if I didn't drag you away from the reception that would be it. We'd never have a chance to talk.'

'I assumed you'd be going back with the rest of the Brits tomorrow.'

'I'm flying to Boston tomorrow. I'm on leave at Harvard this term.'

There is silence apart from the crashing of waves. We stand, side by side, looking over the ocean towards North America. 'Off to the New World,' I say eventually. 'Like Christopher Columbus.' There is a tight band around my throat and my voice is scratchy.

'Except that he went for a little bit longer than me. I'm coming back for a few days at Thanksgiving. There's something I wanted to ask you, Sally.'

'Ask away.'

'Perhaps we could go out for dinner when I come back. Get to know each other. It's a couple of months away, I know . . . '

I steal a look at him. He is still gazing towards America. Lightly I touch his arm and he turns to look at me. 'I'd love to. Perhaps you might phone me before then though?'

But neither of us can find a pen or a phone. We scrabble through our pockets and I search my bag in vain. I think of running into the hotel to retrieve my mobile but why waste these last few moments before Anthony leaves. I explain that my home number is unlisted but he reminds me that he can easily find my work number online. Then he kisses the tip of my nose. 'I've wanted to do that since yesterday,' he says, laughing.

I touch my nose with my forefinger; a butterfly caress, like Anthony's kiss. His face is glowing in the evening light. The red-gold disc of the sun slips down the sky and casts a blazing ladder of reflections onto the sea. Perhaps we are starting a voyage; perhaps I am finishing a voyage; who knows what might happen.

When he goes, I don't turn to watch. I keep my eyes on the sun as it sinks below the horizon.

5

THEN

When my father collected me for the second time at Redruth Station he seemed so much older than he had nearly a week ago. Charlie and I had fled London the week before, and had been staying with my parents for only a few days before I realised I needed to go back to London to collect a crucial bundle of notes that I'd forgotten and that I needed to finish writing up my thesis. It hadn't been a pleasant trip and I'd been so glad to see my father again, waiting on the platform at Redruth to meet me. But I'd swear his skin was greyer than it had been when he'd collected Charlie and me those few days earlier, and there were lines on his face that I'd never noticed before. Or maybe I just hadn't looked at him properly, so absorbed was I in my own worries.

My mother didn't seem too good either. Only for Charlie was she managing to keep a bright voice and smile. This hurt more than I thought it could; that she was trying so hard. But Charlie was still treating the trip as a holiday and when she was at the local school my mother spent all her time outside. In the late afternoon, once the light faded and while Charlie was watching a DVD, I caught sight of my mother at the top of the garden, surrounded by a pile of weeds, her arms hanging loosely by her side. For ten minutes she didn't move while the shadows lengthened around her. She just stood there, staring out to sea, her shoulders folded inwards.

★ ★ ★

It was a complete surprise when the police dropped by. I was glad my father answered the door and not my mother. We were in the garden having breakfast when they rang the front doorbell. My father went inside and a few moments later fetched me in; I carried my half-empty mug of coffee with me. He led me not to the sitting room but to his study. That seemed odd. Two police officers, a woman and a man, stood awkwardly in front of the desk, as if waiting for a dressing-down by the headmaster. The woman was young, barely twenty-five, and looked as if she was growing out of her uniform, while the man, who was around forty, I would guess, was holding in front of him his peaked cap with the black and white chequered band around it. He introduced himself as Sergeant Trevellyan. Both officers refused to take a seat when my father offered. Avoiding their serious faces, I glanced around the room. It was then that I noticed that the newspapers from earlier in the week were piled on top of one of the bookcases, well out of Charlie's reach. My agitation grew and my hand began to shake. Carefully I put down my coffee mug on my father's desk.

'We need to speak to Mrs Hector alone,' the taller one said when my father looked as if he was about to shut the door and make himself comfortable. The man had a gentle voice and a strong local accent. After my father had gone, he suggested I sit. Once I did so, a few seconds passed when all I could hear was the ticking of the clock on the mantelpiece and the heavy breathing of the older police officer. Through the open window I could see Charlie piling grass clippings onto an old tray, while my parents sat, talking intently, on a faded garden bench. A seagull flew overhead, its call evoking happier memories of long summers by the sea.

'I'm sorry to have to tell you, Mrs Hector, that your husband's been found dead in London,' Sergeant Trevellyan said.

'That's impossible,' I said. 'He's barely thirty-one and very fit. And I saw him only a few days ago.' I'd been trying to blank out that day but now I ripped aside the frail fabric of forgetfulness and resuscitated the memory. Surely what had happened to Jeff then couldn't have killed him. He'd been on his feet and out the front door of my building in a flash.

'I'm afraid it's the truth.' The policeman's voice had become even more soothing.

My throat felt constricted. I took a deep breath before saying, 'Why haven't the London police contacted me?'

'It's protocol. The Met called us and that's why we're here. It has to be done face-to-face, you see.'

There was a pause. I could hear my heartbeat pounding in my inner ear. I said, 'Where did my husband die?'

'At the flat of a friend, apparently. Someone called Steve James.' There was another pause before he added, 'I understand you're separated from your husband.'

'I am.'

'Did you know that he took drugs?'

I answered that I didn't. The policeman explained that it looked as if Jeff had died from complications from a head injury that were made worse by a cocktail of drugs and drink. I guessed what this meant. That the bang on his head that he got when he fell must have been preceded by — or maybe followed up by — substance abuse.

'The Met want you to go up to London to identify the body and you'll be needed for an interview.'

This would be my second journey up to London this week and I couldn't bear the thought of it. I tried to focus on the ghastliness of the train journey rather than on what I would find at the other end. The policeman gave me some procedural details about where to go and who to report to. I scribbled his instructions on a piece of blank paper that I found on my father's desk. Having something to do with my hands was one way of concealing my anxiety. It didn't stop the queasiness though. The coffee in the mug I'd put down earlier smelled revolting and I held my breath as I shifted it onto one of the bookshelves.

No sooner had the police officers gone than Zoë rang.

'I'm so sorry, darling,' she said. 'I'm so terribly sorry this has happened.'

I mumbled some response.

'When are you coming up to London?'

'This afternoon.'

'They'll have to interview each of us again.'

'I know.'

'Sally, can I see you?'

'If you must but I saw you only a few days ago.' My voice sounded cracked and I swallowed to clear my throat. If only my head could be so easily cleared. It felt as if it were stuffed with cotton wool that was slowing down my thought processes.

'We barely spoke that time.' Zoë's voice sounded too loud and I wanted her off the phone.

'It was for long enough.'

'Well, we both know what happened.'

'So do the CID.' That interview only days before had gone on and on.

'We just don't know what happened afterwards. Did they tell you anything?'

'Only that he probably died of a drug overdose and a head injury. What did they tell you?'

'Much the same.'

After replacing the receiver, I saw through the window that Charlie had filled two small plastic dishes with grass clippings, and was carrying them to her grandparents. I heard her clear voice saying, 'This is your pretend lunch and I'm in charge.' My mother laughed at this; the first time I'd heard her laugh for days.

She wouldn't be too happy when she learned I had to go to London again, and why.

6

NOW

'Hello!' Zoë calls from the bottom of the steps leading up to our front door. 'I'm sorry I'm late.'

Charlie and I meet her on the landing. She's wearing a fine wool charcoal trouser suit, which sets off to great advantage her cropped platinum blonde hair. She kisses Charlie first, on both cheeks, 'Mwah-mwah,' and afterwards adds one more, 'mwah.'

'Dutch style,' she says. 'I've just come back from Amsterdam, literally this minute, straight from the airport.' She hands Charlie a bottle of wine. 'Here's something to take your mind off work. And something sweet for later,' she says, giving me a large paper bag. Her shrug is apologetic, as if bringing a present is a gesture I might find unwelcome. She turns back to my daughter, who is beaming at her. 'How grown up you look, Charlie! Just like a model. Lucky you to be so slim. I've always had to watch the calories.'

'Come in out of the rain,' I tell her. It's a wet Thursday evening and people are scurrying along the footpath, bent into their umbrellas as much for protection against the wind as the rain. In the face of this weather, it's hard to imagine that Vigo was little more than a week ago.

Next it's my turn for Zoë's inspection. 'Sally,

you're looking gorgeous. How clever to have those colours together. That yellow shirt with the red trousers looks fabulous with your hair.' Zoë has the gift of making everyone she talks to feel wonderful. I threw on my clothes today more or less at random.

'Tonight I'm celebrating,' Zoë says.

'What?' Charlie asks.

'My new man.'

'What was wrong with Jon?' Charlie's voice is pitched higher than usual. 'You haven't gone and ditched him, have you?'

'All over, darling.'

'You've only been with him a few months.' Charlie finds Zoë slightly shocking, as I did once. Charlie would hate it if I behaved like Zoë, but Zoë's behaviour augments rather than diminishes Charlie's fascination with her.

Zoë waves an arm, the gesture theatrical. 'Didn't I tell you?' She knows full well that she hasn't, and she pauses for effect. 'Jon and I broke up last month, not long after I met this really dishy Dutch man in Amsterdam. It was love at first sight.'

'Well, I hope you're practising safe sex,' says Charlie darkly, as if she is decades older than Zoë. If Charlie were not my daughter, I would find this role reversal amusing. I look at the pale oval of her lovely face, her delicate features and high cheekbones; she looks like her father when he was young. The dream I had in Vigo flashes back briefly and I push it away. All of a sudden I think of Marge's packet of photos and *things*. They will be on their way to Charlie soon and I

32

still haven't told her what she needs to know about her father.

'Of course I am, Charlie,' says Zoë. 'I have to set you a good example.'

'You're a lousy role model for the youth of today.'

I pour Zoë and Charlie each a glass of wine, and leave them to it, while I dash downstairs to the kitchen to make the final touches to our supper and set the table. How confident Zoë is and how essentially uncomplicated, I think as I dress the salad. She practises serial monogamy except at the point of transition between relationships, when she practises bigamy. In the ten years that I've known her she has had just one period without a man. That was after I first met her and it only lasted four months. She does what she wants, taking on new men and dumping old ones with an extraordinary ruthlessness. Yet as a friend she is one of the most loyal women I have ever met and I love her like a sister.

Sometimes I envy her uncomplicated attitude to sex. I tried to follow her example once. Not immediately after Jeff died, but later. In the first two years after his death I avoided men altogether — apart from my colleagues. When I was nearing thirty and started to go out with men again, I picked them younger than me, men who wouldn't threaten me in any way. And my behaviour was not unlike Zoë's, dating them and then dumping them as soon as anything serious threatened; dumping them before they could dump me. I pretended to myself that I wasn't hurting them; because they were so much younger than me, they must have known it couldn't last. And I never let these men come home, never let them meet Charlie. I used them I suppose, and not solely for pleasure. It was for my ego, to prove that I was still attractive, to prove that I was sexually competent. But once Charlie turned thirteen, once she became an adolescent, I felt obliged to stop this behaviour: it became impossible to do what I would disapprove of her doing. It was at this point that I noticed that all the men of my own age had gone — partnered, married, out of circulation — and unlike Zoë I could never sleep with another woman's partner.

When I join Zoë and Charlie in the living room, I'm surprised to discover that Zoë is still talking about her personal life. Charlie is hanging on to Zoë's every word.

'You'll never guess what I found out about Jon.' Zoë's voice is almost a whisper, although I can hear her clearly from the door. She leans towards Charlie, their two blonde heads almost touching. This is Zoë's conspiratorial way of talking, and one that she often adopts. It flatters listeners into believing that they are the uniquely chosen recipients of her confidences. She says, 'You know how clever Jon is. Surely I've told you about all those lovely notes he used to leave?'

Charlie nods, but Zoë tells us again. 'I'd find yellow Post-it stickers all around my flat, with bits of love poetry on them.' She sighs. 'I kept them all of course. I'm such a romantic.' She pauses, while I refill her wine glass. 'Not long after I told him it was over,' she continues, 'I packed up his things and took them to his flat.'

34

Zoë may seem like a romantic, but she is first and foremost a realist. She refuses to let any man move in with her; she is frightened she would lose her independence. But she does allow them to leave a few possessions in her flat. 'He wasn't in, but I still had his keys, although we hardly ever met there. So I let myself in and thought that while I was there I might as well have a quick look around.'

'You snooped.'

'No, Charlie, I just wanted to see if I'd left any of my stuff there. And do you know what I found?'

She pauses for breath and opens her large, almost-black eyes very wide.

'What?' Charlie and I chorus.

'A book of love quotations on his desk. He'd got all those things out of a book.'

Her laughter is so infectious it's impossible not to join in. 'Never trust the romantic ones, darlings,' she says, wiping away tears of mirth.

'Does it matter that he hadn't written them himself? He did love you, after all.'

'It matters because I thought he'd made them up, and he knew that.' Zoë is emphatic on this point. Over the years I've learned that she has high standards, and ones that are not always predictable. 'That's plagiarism, isn't it?'

'True. But he wasn't sitting an exam. He was just telling you his feelings.'

'Let's not talk of exams with poor Charlie suffering so.' Zoë smiles sympathetically at Charlie. 'What else have you been up to? Any more all-night orgies like the one you had when your mum was in Spain?' Zoë winks, but it's not clear whether this is directed at Charlie or me.

'Just the usual. Drugs, sex and rock 'n' roll.'

'Is that all?'

'Isn't that enough? Don't you start putting pressure on me to rebel. Like, Mum's been doing that ever since I turned sixteen.'

Dinner is almost over when the phone rings. 'For you, Charlie,' I say automatically, but she is already on her way to the extension upstairs.

'Charlie's working really hard,' I tell Zoë. 'Thank God things were easier in my day. I don't remember studying much for the A-levels, and I still got into the university I wanted.'

'Don't be so smug.' Zoë pours us each more wine. 'That was nearly twenty years ago. You've probably forgotten how hard you worked.'

'I'll never forget the exams. My stomach was growling all through the maths paper and I was covered in a ghastly rash the whole time.'

'There you are. Different people react differently. I'm glad I wasn't a don's daughter. The pressure on Charlie must be enormous.'

'Self-imposed.'

'She adores you, Sally. And she knows what will please you.'

'I've never suggested she goes to university.'

'But it's all implicit these days. I was lucky. No-one in my family had done GCSE maths before me, so they all thought I was a genius when I got a B. Relatives kept taking me to one side and slipping me five quid. That's why I went on to do A-levels.'

Zoë clears the table while I make coffee. 'You're

looking very well,' she says, while I load up the tray with the cafetière and some cups. 'Not that you don't normally of course. Has something happened? How are you getting on with that shrink of yours?'

'Helen? I'd like to talk about Jeff but I haven't had the opportunity yet.'

'I thought you made the opportunities. Isn't that what it's all about? You don't get only one chance at happiness, Sally. You've got to get the past out of your system.'

'I'll get round to it.'

'If the sessions aren't going anywhere, why've you been looking so pleased with yourself all evening?'

'Have I?' I can feel a surge of blood working up my neck and into my cheeks. 'You don't miss much. I met a rather nice man last week. About my age, well, a little bit older. The nicest I've met for some time.' I wonder why I'm telling Zoë this. Part of me wants to forget Anthony. He is attractive but threatening too, threatening to the fragile equilibrium I've reached over the past few years. And maybe he is just too perfect.

'At last. Well, what are you going to do about it?'

'Wait and see.'

'Do get on with your life, Sally. Charlie's almost an adult and you've done a terrific job bringing her up. But she'll be gone soon. It's time to consider your own future.'

'You sound like my mother.'

'A very sensible woman, I've always thought. What's he like?'

Briefly I describe Anthony, leaving out the bits about how appealing I found him. I don't want to tell her too much in case nothing ever comes of this.

'He sounds very suitable. I'd like to meet him.'

'He's gone off to Harvard for four months, so that'll be a bit difficult.'

'Oh darling, you do pick them! Did you find that out before or after you decided you fancied him?'

'Cheap psychology, Zoë.' Though I smile at her, I feel confused, rocked by opposing emotions: wanting to see Anthony again but at the same time wanting to avoid what might follow. Wanting to see him again but wanting to avoid being hurt if he doesn't contact me. While he promised on the terrace in Vigo to call me, what if he doesn't? That evening I should have made the effort to find a pen to write down my phone number instead of simply agreeing with his suggestion that he check me out online.

After Zoë leaves, I go outside. The rain has stopped but the steps leading into our garden are wet. I turn the back doormat upside down and sit on the side that is relatively dry. Anthony surfaces in my mind, like a piece of music that I can't get out of my head. Charlie's elderly cat, Tico, wraps himself around my legs and purrs loudly while I rub him behind his ears.

When the phone rings I jump to my feet but it turns out to be next door's. In a year's time Charlie will be going to university. And when she goes, there will be a gaping hole in my life.

7

THEN

From the train, Charlie and I had watched the sun sink below the horizon, a dark red ball veiled in a haze of evening mist. Earlier that afternoon I'd collected Charlie from school and whisked her and our kitten, Tico, off to catch the train to Cornwall to stay with my parents. I had to get out of London; I couldn't bear the thought of being contacted by journalists. And I couldn't bear the thought that Jeff might try to see Charlie and me. On the train, after we'd opened the packets of sandwiches I'd bought for the journey, I told Charlie that we wouldn't be sticking with the last name of Hector. I was researching under the name of Lachlan and things would get too confusing otherwise. Of course I didn't tell her that the real purpose was to confer anonymity, so the press couldn't track us down. So Charlie became Charlotte Hector Lachlan, but of course she never told anyone that was her name, because even a young school kid knows that double-barrelled names set you apart somehow, and she never wanted to be set apart. From that time on she was simply Charlotte Lachlan.

'I like being here,' Charlie had said that first evening in Coverack when I was tucking her into bed in the attic room. Although the heavy

39

curtains were drawn, we could hear the waves as they gently shifted the shingle along the shoreline. 'How long are we going to stay, Mummy?'

'I don't know yet, Charlie. It might be a while.'

'Will I go to school here?'

'Yes. Tomorrow if you like.'

'Cool. I'll make new friends and one of them might have a boat.' Boats were her current obsession since watching a few episodes of *Elias the Little Rescue Boat*.

'Sleep well, my darling.' I kissed her brow.

'What will you do, Mummy?'

'Finish my thesis.' But I'd realised only half an hour ago that I'd left a box-file full of some crucial notes in the London flat. That meant I'd have to go back again to collect it.

'Can Tico sleep on my bed?'

'Yes, but keep the door closed so he doesn't run away.'

My parents were sitting in the living room when I came downstairs. My spirits plummeted when I saw three newspapers in a row on the coffee table. They hadn't been there before. On the front page of each was a photo of that woman.

Zoë had been photographed getting out of a taxi. Although she was raising a briefcase to shield her head, the photographer had caught her in the instant before. Her face was unmistakably bruised and swollen. In *The Times* there was also a small picture of Jeff. His features were blurred, as if he'd been moving when the photo was taken. His hair was flopping forward onto his forehead.

I sat on the sofa next to my mother. The

40

upholstery was too soft and I could feel my body sinking into it. With unsteady hands, I picked up the paper and read the text.

ISLINGTON DESIGNER CHARGED WITH ASSAULTING ZOE

A man has been arrested and taken to Maida Vale Police Station charged with assaulting the glamorous presenter of Rearranging Lives.

Zoë McIntyre, aged 29, was admitted to hospital two days ago with a possible fractured cheekbone after an incident at a London restaurant.

It is alleged that Mr Jeffrey Hector, aged 31, punched his lover Zoë in the face several times before smashing a chair through the window of the restaurant.

After her release from hospital, Zoë said she would not be taking any time off work: 'I'm not going to let anything like this hold up my show, and I intend to press charges. Violence against women is something that can never be condoned.'

My mother coughed. There were tears in her eyes and her hand was shaking when she put it on my arm. 'Sally,' she said. 'Did Jeff . . . did he ever . . . to you?'

'Yes.' I felt suddenly cold and began to shiver. Before I knew it I was clutching a glass of Scotch and there was a rug over my knees. My mother was holding my hand in hers. I must have fallen asleep soon after.

Later that evening, the phone rang when my

parents were pottering about in the kitchen. I picked up the receiver in the living room.

'Have you seen the papers?' Jeff said.

I took a deep breath and thought of hanging up. 'Yes,' I said. 'That's why I brought Charlie down here.'

'Zoë's taking me to court.'

'How could you do it, Jeff?'

'She deserved it, the bitch.'

It didn't seem to occur to him that I mightn't take his side. 'Why did she deserve it?' My throat felt as if there were an iron band around it and I had to make an effort to breathe. In the kitchen my parents were talking still and I wondered what they were saying. My mother's voice was muted and my father's was a staccato accompaniment. The anger in Dad's voice was for Jeff; he was never cross with my mother.

'She dented the new BMW along one side,' Jeff said. 'It wouldn't have been so bad if she'd apologised but she didn't. She just laughed.'

'I think she's right to take you to court.' I found it easy to be honest when he was at the other end of a telephone line and not standing right next to me. 'You can't go around bashing up people because they do something you don't like.'

But he was convinced he'd done nothing wrong. He thought that he was simply teaching Zoë a lesson. She wasn't badly hurt, he told me. She deserved what she got; she provoked him.

'But she's seriously injured.' I thought of her bruised face, the cut eyebrow, the eye that she had trouble opening, the abrasion on her cheekbone.

42

'The newspapers exaggerate. You can't believe anything you read. This is a godsend, for them and for Zoë. It'll boost their sales and Zoë's viewing figures.'

He hesitated, and I wondered if he realised how cynical he was sounding. But it seemed he was merely pausing for breath in order to continue with his lamentation. 'I'm the only sucker that comes out of this badly,' he said. 'Nobody's mentioned how poorly Zoë behaved.'

Again I thought of hanging up and again I decided against it. The last thing I wanted was a custody battle with Jeff, not that he would have a chance of winning that. But I felt I had to keep the lines of communication open between us. I asked him if his father had read the newspaper accounts. But his father was abroad; he and Jeff's stepmother, Marge, had emigrated to Australia two years before so there was some possibility that he mightn't find out at all, or at least not for a time.

While Jeff cared what his father might think, it became obvious as his monologue proceeded that his primary concern was that his design practice might be adversely affected by the publicity. But after a time it occurred to him that perhaps the notoriety might bring in more clients. I gritted my teeth. Maybe not the women, he said; but yes, he thought it might actually bring in the men.

His voice had become so loud that I had to hold the receiver away from my head. Scents from the garden wafted through the open window — from the recently mown grass and

43

the roses in the garden bed. My fingers were becoming sore from clutching the receiver too hard: I was transferring my anger with Jeff to my hand.

He began to tell me what a ghastly night he'd had in the police cells. In that interminable phone conversation, he never once asked after Charlie. It was as if she didn't exist.

Although I wasn't at all sympathetic, that didn't stop him. He denied causing injury; he denied any responsibility. His view was that he was the victim and that he, rather than Zoë, deserved pity. After he'd got all that off his chest, he told me he was planning a few nights out. He and his old school friend, Steve James, were going to get pissed. They planned a bit of a bender; that was how he went on to describe it. They were going to celebrate Jeff getting bailed out of jail.

I don't think he heard much of what I was saying. He was talking for his own benefit, to justify his behaviour to himself. As soon as I put down the receiver, I realised he was using neutralisation techniques. Deny the injury took place. That way you couldn't be held responsible for something because it hadn't occurred.

There was no doubt that he was getting worse, not better.

8

NOW

'Has the stuff from Marge arrived yet, Charlie?' I dump my briefcase on the floor by the door and shrug off my raincoat.

'It'll take a couple of weeks,' Charlie says, blowing me a kiss. There is a steaming cup of coffee on the table in front of her. 'I only wrote to her a few days ago. You know what the post from Australia is like.'

Keeping my face expressionless, I stroll to the bay window. The street is deserted, save for a young man sauntering along the pavement as if it's a warm summer's evening and not a blustery late October night with scraps of leaves flying about like confetti. He sees me and waves. I recognise him now; he lives two doors away.

'Are you worried it might get lost, Ma? Marge said she was going to send it registered post.'

'No. I was just wondering if it had come.'

'I'll tell you when it gets here.'

'Thanks. I'd hate for it to get lost.' What a hypocrite I'm being; I'd love the parcel to get lost. I'm dreading what might be in it and I want to be in the house when it arrives.

And I've simply got to let Charlie know the truth about how her father died.

* * *

When I had arrived back at Coverack, some days after identifying Jeff's body in London and more ghastly interviews afterwards, I found Charlie playing outside in the back garden. Watched by my mother, she was crawling about on her hands and knees in the grass, absorbed in some game involving half a dozen clothes pegs and a few stones.

'Come into Grandpa's study,' I said, after we'd hugged and kissed. Charlie's body was hot from her exertions and she smelled of recently mown grass and clean cotton. After sitting her down in one of the armchairs in my father's study, I knelt on the Persian rug in front of her. 'Charlie, your father's had a massive heart attack.' I took her hands in mine. They were warm and sticky. 'He died peacefully, in his sleep.' I wanted to observe her reaction, to gauge what she might feel so that I could better protect her from what was happening to us.

But Charlie didn't seem to feel anything. It was the shock, I suppose. But I knew I'd have to be careful with her: it might take days or even months before she understood the loss. She said, 'What's a massive heart attack?'

I explained that it was when the heart stopped pumping blood around the body, as if the body's engine had been suddenly switched off. 'Your dad wouldn't have felt any pain,' I said, 'because he was asleep. But you mustn't worry about it happening to you when you fall asleep, because it hardly ever happens to anyone until they're well over sixty.'

I didn't take Charlie to her father's funeral.

She stayed with my parents while I caught the train up to Somerset, to the seaside town of Burnham-on-Sea where Jeff was to be buried, and where he had grown up. The arrangements for the funeral were made quickly, almost furtively, once the coroner reached her verdict of accidental death. There were only six of us there: Jeff's father, a couple of his friends from school whom I hadn't met before, Zoë and me, and the clergyman. Jeff's father had flown back from Australia as soon as he'd heard the news.

★ ★ ★

Standing at the bay window in my house in Kentish Town, I begin to shiver as the wind roughly fingers the window sashes. From the creaking of the floorboards behind me, I guess that Charlie is now in front of the bookcase. She is probably looking at the silver-framed photograph of the three of us that was taken not long after she turned four. I keep it there, on the middle bookshelf, for Charlie. Although I never look at it myself, I will always remember it. In the picture, Charlie is wearing the Liberty dress that my mother gave her and her hair is smooth and shiny. Standing in the middle of a park bench on Hampstead Heath, she is framed by her father and me. We are all smiling for the camera. We are the perfect family.

I pull the curtains across the rattling window sashes. October is the worst month for gales.

9

THEN

My friend Alessandra had taken Charlie to see *Peter Pan*. It was a few months after Jeff and I had separated, and I'd hoped for an uninterrupted afternoon working on my thesis. Alessandra was a fellow graduate student who liked to borrow Charlie from time to time and, as Charlie adored her, this arrangement worked well for all of us.

I had just settled down at the kitchen table with my laptop when the phone rang. It reverberated through the draughty unheated hallway of my flat. Reluctantly I got up to answer it.

'Hello, is that Sally?' I didn't recognise the deep female voice at the end of the line.

'Yes.'

'It's Jeff's friend here.' She paused. Right away I knew who she was but I didn't intend to help her out. 'His girlfriend,' she added.

'I see,' I said, as coldly as possible.

'Something dreadful has happened.' She hesitated again. 'I can't really explain on the phone. Can you come around?'

'Is it about Jeff?'

'Yes. But he's not ill or anything. I need to talk to you. As soon as possible.'

'What about right now.'

'I can't explain over the phone. Can't you come round?'

There was a pause. 'I'd rather not,' I said.

'Oh, I'm sorry; you've got your little daughter. Shall I come to your place instead? I could get a cab right away. Though Charlie shouldn't really hear what I have to say.'

'No, don't do that.' I didn't want this woman in my flat. 'I'll come and see you. Charlie's with a friend at the moment.'

'Thank God for that.'

'I'll be there in an hour.'

'Thanks Sally. That's really very sweet of you.' She gave me her address in Little Venice before ringing off.

I changed quickly; call it vanity, call it self-respect, but I didn't want to meet Jeff's girlfriend wearing my scruffy working clothes. I caught the tube to Warwick Avenue station and walked the short distance — through wide, tree-lined streets and past affluent-looking houses — to the address she'd given me. This turned out to be a mansion block of flats overlooking the canal. I pressed the button on the entry-phone. No one spoke to me but the door sprang open almost immediately and I walked up one flight of stairs. By now I was feeling decidedly curious. The door to flat 4 was ajar. As I crossed the landing it opened to reveal a slender woman, perhaps ten centimetres taller than me. At first I couldn't see her face: she appeared to be dressed in black from head-to-toe, and was silhouetted against the bright light blazing out of her flat.

'Come in.' She stood back to let me by, and shut the front door behind me. When she turned,

I saw her face fully illuminated for the first time. The shock took my breath away. There was an abrasion on her left cheekbone and a small cut immediately above the ocular orbit; the flesh around this was so bruised and swollen that she could barely open that eye. Even with this damage, I could see that she was beautiful, with classically proportioned features. Horrified, throat suddenly constricted, I opened and shut my mouth but couldn't get any words out.

Of course I knew without being told who was responsible.

'I'm not an attractive sight,' she said. 'Thanks for coming, Sally. You can see why I didn't want to go out looking like this.'

I followed her into a large sunlit room overlooking the canal. Her shiny platinum hair, cropped very short, glowed like an aura. 'I'm sorry, I've just realised that I haven't told you my name,' she said, turning to look at me. Her battered face was even more shocking in this pristine room. 'I'm Zoë. Zoë McIntyre.'

The name rang a bell, yet I'd never heard Jeff mention it. I thought I'd seen her face somewhere before, although I couldn't remember where. Clearly she expected some sort of recognition. She looked faintly disappointed when I didn't react, when I simply said, 'Hello, Zoë.'

'Do sit down,' she said.

I sat in the Eames chair she indicated, and she perched on the edge of the white upholstered sofa opposite. 'When did it happen?' I asked, leaning forward. To relax back into this chair would put me at a disadvantage.

'Last night.'

'How?'

'Oh, surely you can guess how it happened. Jeff lost his temper. He didn't like something I did. But instead of talking it through like a mature adult, he lashed out at me like some stupid schoolboy bully. He punched me and when I fell over, he kicked me really hard in the stomach.'

'Your poor face.' I almost apologised, but realised at once that this was inappropriate. I wasn't responsible for Jeff; I was never responsible for Jeff. He was not my fault.

'The whole thing took place in public. In a bloody restaurant, can you believe? The man's mad.'

This marked a new stage in Jeff's violence. My throat felt dry. I swallowed and could hear the gulp.

'You'll be wondering why I wanted to see you. It wasn't to get your sympathy. I know you must really hate me.' Zoë spoke almost aggressively and I could see a pulse jumping in the hollow at the base of her throat.

'Was this the first time?' I had to find out if he had begun with this, or with a less extreme form of violence, as he had done with me.

'Of course it was. Do you think I would have put up with this and hung around for more?' she said irritably. 'But what I want to know is; did he ever hit you?'

'Yes.' A nerve under my eye twitched. Although I smoothed the skin with my forefinger, it jerked again and again.

'How often?'

'I suppose every six months or so.'

She raised one eyebrow, the undamaged one, before smiling oddly, the way people sometimes do in the face of bad news. From these grimaces I intuited that she thought little of me, a woman who'd let herself be knocked around. She said, 'More fool you for putting up with it.'

I stood, my eye convulsing again in a way that must surely have been noticeable. Anger made my heart pound too hard and it was a struggle to keep my voice steady when I spoke. 'I'm not hanging around here listening to your abuse,' I said. 'You're a bitch, if you don't mind me saying so. You stole my husband and now, when he turns out to be a bad draw, you start bawling me out. I think you deserve everything you got!'

'Well, at least I'm not some pathetic little woman, standing by her man regardless of whether he's a dickhead or not.' She kept her voice calm and rather patronising, as if she was speaking to a small child. But my anger drained away when I saw that talking was an effort for her: that pulse at the base of her neck was thumping still. She turned away, perhaps wanting to conceal her emotion, but a few seconds later she continued, still in that condescending tone, 'And he really is a dickhead, darling. In fact, he's more than that, he's a . . . he's a . . . ' She paused, at a loss for words.

'Wanker,' I supplied.

We looked at each other. For the first time since I had come into the room we looked properly at each other, peering deep into each other's eyes. Hers were a very dark brown, so dark as to be almost black, although I could barely see her left eye so puffed up was the surrounding flesh. She held my gaze for perhaps half a minute. Then she said: 'I'm so sorry, Sally. Do please sit down again. I've been incredibly insensitive.'

So I sat on the edge of the black leather Eames chair, and told her the history of Jeff's violence.

When I'd finished, she said, 'I think we need a glass of wine, Sally, before we go any further.'

While she was in the kitchen, I inspected my surroundings. The polished wooden floor was covered with an orange and red Persian carpet; the two huge sofas were upholstered in a coarse white fabric that I would find impossible to keep clean; the white-painted walls were hung with three or four vivid abstract paintings; the windows were uncurtained. The whole effect was of light and a minimalist good taste that would appeal to Jeff.

Zoë reappeared after a few minutes with a tray holding a bottle of white wine, beaded with condensation, and two glasses.

'Where's Jeff now?' I asked.

'Maida Vale Police Station. He's been charged with assault.'

I inhaled sharply. Zoë had the courage to do something that I hadn't and I felt a reluctant admiration for her. Then I thought of my daughter, and said, 'Charlie mustn't hear any of this.'

'I've already laid charges against him.'

'You can drop them.'

'I won't drop them. He's a bastard. This is the only way he'll be made to stop thinking he can bash up any woman he's on with, just because she does something he doesn't like.'

'But we have to protect Charlie.'

'Protect Charlie? Too right we do. For heaven's sake, Sally, Jeff could have started beating up Charlie too. Didn't you ever think of that? You're an intelligent woman; surely that's crossed your mind.'

Intelligent but blind. Why had I never thought of this? Possibly because I had judged his actions as sexual when perhaps they were not.

'I'm afraid it's too late to back out,' Zoë said.

She handed me a copy of the *News of the World*. The paper had been folded over to reveal a picture of Zoë: her face was damaged and one eye shut. She was looking directly at the photographer when the picture was taken, defiantly holding her head high. I read the caption underneath: ZOË'S ZAPPED. I read on: *The glamorous TV presenter of* Rearranging Lives *was assaulted last night. Police are holding a man for questioning.* The rest of the article was devoted to Zoë. The assailant's name wasn't mentioned, and there was no photo of Jeff.

'I didn't realise you worked for TV,' I said. This was a most unfortunate development, and for the moment I couldn't see any way around it. Even if Zoë were not to press charges, there would still be a lot of publicity, and it was almost inevitable that Jeff's name would be revealed sooner or later. Probably sooner.

'You haven't seen me on the box?' Zoë's tone was incredulous.

'I don't watch TV. I'm trying to finish my PhD so I don't have much spare time.'

'Oh, Jeff did mention something about that. But you can see my point. It's too late to turn back.'

'But you could drop the charges, Zoë. I know it's too late to stop the media. But if you don't press charges, there won't be any court case. We've got to protect Charlie from all the publicity. We've got to do something.'

'We'll think of a way.' She topped up my barely-touched wine glass, and poured another for herself. I was worried by this new development. If Charlie were not already attending school, she could have used my surname instead of Jeff's; that would have afforded her some protection. Was it too late for that now? It would be hard to take her off to school on Monday with a new name when the school had known her by Jeff's surname for the last two years.

After a while, Zoë said, 'The damage has already been done, from Charlie's perspective. The media are onto it. And I've decided not to take time off work, at least not much. The show can go on. So there's going to be a fuss whether I drop charges or not.'

'But there'll be less of a fuss if you drop charges. Think of it from Charlie's point of view.'

'But there are lots of Hectors in London. Why should anyone at school think Charlie's father is Jeff Hector?'

'There'll be photographs. Stuff on the TV

news. Someone at her school will find out. And kids can be so cruel.' And how would Charlie feel about finding out her father could be violent? It would be hard for her to cope with that.

'I'm sorry, Sally. This can be a lesson to him. We might prevent other women being hurt and even Charlie, in the future. And anyway, shouldn't she come to terms with what her father's really like?'

I could understand Zoë's point of view. She was brave and she was angry, and I could see that she was determined too. Maybe I could move away from London for a while, give Charlie my last name. Charlie and I could stay at my parent's house in Cornwall. They would love that, and Charlie could go to school there until all the fuss had died down. I could take my work with me. I was on the writing-up stage and no longer needed to use the laboratory, so that would be relatively easy. In fact Charlie and I should leave for Cornwall first thing in the morning; I'd pack up some of our stuff that very night. I was determined to shelter Charlie from learning about Jeff for as long as possible.

I left Zoë's flat shortly afterwards, when we'd reached a decision of sorts. Zoë agreed to do all that she could to keep Jeff's name out of the media. We both knew there was probably little chance she'd succeed. I gave her my parents' phone number in Cornwall. She insisted on calling a taxi for me and — when it arrived — she came down to see me off. Before I could prevent her, she prepaid the driver.

'I know this is difficult for you,' Zoë said, as we stood side-by-side on the pavement next to the waiting cab. A chilling evening light angled across the quiet street and cast long shadows. Opposite us, parked cars were arranged like text between the punctuation marks of the plane trees. The only sign of life was the distant swishing of traffic from the Edgware Road.

As Zoë kissed my cheek, she said, 'If I'd thought you were still together when I met Jeff, I wouldn't have slept with him.'

'I bet,' I thought, before squeezing her hand and climbing into the taxi.

10

At a quarter to eight, I get off the bus at South End Green, into fine rain. The flower-vendor is setting up his stall. Water drips off the canvas awning onto massed bunches of carnations and lilies trucked in from the Netherlands.

My shoes are damp, and I'm getting cold feet about what to tell Helen. When I ring the doorbell, her voice on the intercom tells me to enter. The waiting room is as tidy as always; the carpet light beige and spotless, the sofa and armchairs upholstered in a terracotta-coloured coarse-weave fabric. The ormolu clock on the mantelpiece shows ten minutes to eight. I am early again.

Apprehension begins to nibble at the edges of my resolve. From my perch on the edge of an armchair, I can view the hallway. Never once have I seen a member of Helen's household. I used to occupy the waiting time by speculating about her private life, but this is no longer distraction enough. After unfolding my damp newspaper, I flick through the pages. *US to put climate change 'front and center' of diplomatic efforts, Kerry vows; An Alaskan TV reporter makes an on-air exit to fight for pot legalization: Fuck it, I quit, she says; William Hague throws down gauntlet to Labour over Scottish MPs' voting rights; Police force must rid itself of predatory men, says Commissioner.*

Now I hear a door upstairs open, followed by the thudding of feet down the stairs. A middle-aged man in a grey suit hurries past. He looks so smart, so much in control, that it's hard to imagine why he needs to see Helen.

Maybe I look like that too, in control of my life.

After a few more minutes Helen comes downstairs. She is taller than me, and handsome, with a square tanned face and bobbed silver hair.

'How are you?' She smiles but doesn't wait for an answer. She turns and trips quickly up the stairs again. Following close behind, I admire her narrow feet, well-shod in shiny black pumps.

Her consulting room is directly over the waiting room and decorated in the same style. There is a thick white envelope on the coffee table. It is propped up against a square glass vase, in which heavily scented red roses are symmetrically arranged. My name is inscribed on the envelope, in black ink, in Helen's elegant writing. It's a work of art, my monthly account. Always left discreetly next to the flowers.

Under the bay window is a sofa that I lie on during our sessions. Helen sits in a matching chair immediately behind my head. She can see my face if she wants to, but I can't see hers.

At once I lie down and urge myself to get on with what I decided to tell her. But in spite of my earlier resolution, I can't bring myself to talk about Jeff. Like the Alaskan reporter, I could shout, 'Fuck it, I quit!' before walking right out of here. Although tempted, I lie still. Although tempted, I say nothing. Is it through nervousness

59

or stubbornness? I can't decide which. The silence continues; the silence grows until it becomes a palpable presence filling the room and obstructing my thoughts.

'Perhaps you want to tell me some more about your marriage,' Helen says, after I've been lying speechless for some minutes.

'Yes and no.' I examine my hands. There are particles of dirt under two of my fingernails, traces of gardening last weekend. It's too early in the day to talk about Jeff. I don't want to be here. I should be at my office. I should be anywhere but here.

I look at my watch: it's eight-thirty. These minutes of muteness in Helen's Hampstead rooms have cost me thirty pounds. I am about to speak when I hear a thumping of footsteps down the stairs; the front door clicks open and is slammed shut again. Stop looking for distractions, I tell myself. Spit out the past and talk. Tell Helen something. Tell her anything. Everything.

'I met a man recently,' I say, a random thought. 'I really liked him.'

'Hmm.' Helen's voice sounds non-committal, or perhaps she is offering encouragement. It must be dull for her to sit with a patient who doesn't speak.

'And do you know what I realised about him? That I recognised him.'

I pause, but Helen doesn't respond. For some reason I think of Celia, and a moment later of my mother. I haven't seen my mother for several months, although we speak on the phone regularly and she will be coming to stay with us in a few weeks' time. I resolve to blurt out to Helen whatever thoughts enter my head and see what she makes of them.

'My parents live in Cornwall on the south coast.' It's strange to me, a scientist, to speak in a stream of consciousness, instead of carefully considering what I'll say before opening my mouth. 'They moved there twelve years ago when my father retired. My mother inherited the house from Celia.' Of course I could be dissembling, trying to avoid talking about Jeff.

Helen crosses her legs; I hear the rasping of her fine nylon tights. Afterwards I hear the sound of pencil on paper. Perhaps she is recording my family tree.

'Celia was my mother's maternal aunt,' I add helpfully. 'My mother was her favourite niece.' Pausing, I wonder what Helen is making of my unstructured remarks. 'Is this relevant, Helen?' My question is motivated by a sense of mischief; I know she won't offer me any guidance but I'm always interested in her reaction.

'That is not for me to say, Sally.' Helen enunciates carefully and, for the first time, I notice that she speaks with a very slight foreign accent; she has over-emphasised the last syllable of my name. 'You will make any connections. Speak as freely as you wish, about whatever you like.'

I restrain a smile: I wouldn't want Helen to think I find her amusing. I begin to rabbit on about my parents, my normal loving parents. My lovely mother who has encouraged me in everything I've chosen to do, apart from that one decision years ago.

'I'm afraid we're going to have to stop there,' Helen says.

I am taken by surprise. Helen stands and glides across the carpet. She opens the door, her smile serene, while I struggle to bring myself back. I get up from the sofa and lurch out of the room, on the way picking up the envelope bearing my name. I fold it in two and slip it into my bag. I'm still stuffing my feet into my shoes as I stumble past Helen.

Outside, the low grey sky is whitening, brightening. I decide to walk along Haverstock Hill Road to Camden Town. The traffic is heavy, and I overtake the crawling cars easily. But I feel exposed on this busy artery, and turn into a quiet side street of terraced houses. Even though it's early October, exuberant plants crowd the small front gardens. This part of Belsize Park is as peaceful as any village.

The character of the streets starts to change as I walk on: there are more flats, and fewer tastefully renovated houses. At Camden Town, the pavements are dirty and there are half a dozen beggars near the entrance to the Tube. One young woman, sitting on the pavement and leaning against the station wall, catches my eye. She is wearing dirty jeans and a low-cut T-shirt, revealing her breasts and a large expanse of blemished unhealthy-looking skin.

'Any spare change for a cup of coffee?' she says.

Probably she will spend any change on drugs, at least so we've been told recently by a cabinet minister. We've all been advised not to give to the beggars on the streets of London. But I drop a couple of pounds into her outstretched hand. This young woman could have been me; she could have been Charlie.

11

NOW

Zoë phones me on Tuesday night, wanting to know if I've made any progress in telling Helen about Jeff.

'I spent the last session talking about my mother's Aunt Celia.'

'Only you can know if that's relevant,' Zoë says, laughing. 'But you did say you'd begin this week.'

'It all takes time. I'm getting ready to tell her, I promise. It's not going to be easy, though.'

'You never thought it would be, did you?'

'I suppose not.'

'Any news from the dream-boat?'

'No. I thought he might have phoned by now, but he hasn't.'

'The cautious academic type. Maybe you should call him.'

'I'll give him till next weekend and try then.' Yet I know I won't do this; my words were merely to keep Zoë quiet. But perhaps if he hasn't phoned me in a couple of weeks' time, I could send him an email.

'There's no way I'd wait this long.'

'I know, Zoë. But that's the way I am. Slow and steady.'

'And that's why we love you, Sal.'

Twelve noon on Wednesday. I have finished two hours of lectures, and have an hour spare to read the papers for the graduate-school board meeting at one o'clock. Kate, one of the administrators, knocks at the door of my office. For a moment I wish I'd locked it: I need the full hour.

'Not disturbing you, am I?' Although Kate's face is oval, the overall effect is of a triangle with its apex in the centre of her forehead. Her mouth is too wide, and its width emphasises that her hazel eyes are too close together. The overall effect is striking and very attractive.

'Not at all.' I find my eyes drifting to the pile of papers on my desk.

Kate grins. 'I've booked you in to see the college photographer next week. Your photo's the only one outstanding on the departmental website.'

'I'll see if I can find an old picture that'll do instead.' I hate having my photograph taken, and if I can find a reasonable one at home I'll save an hour or two during the week as well.

'I've heard that before. You've also got a phone message.' She hands me a piece of paper with a number written on it. 'A Professor Anthony Blake, from Imperial College, but he said he was phoning from the States. You just missed him; he called about twenty minutes ago.'

My heart starts to beat faster. I glance quickly at the slip of paper. 'He's visiting the States. But this is a London number.' I begin to blush, as if

I'm a schoolgirl, and to cover my confusion, I deliberately knock a pencil onto the floor. I don't want the ever-perspicacious Kate to make any inferences about Anthony.

'You've got to stick the area code in front of the number. They're five hours behind,' Kate says while I'm crawling about on the floor under my desk to retrieve the pencil. 'It's the Boston code, 617. He asked if you could call back as soon as possible.'

Kate took me under her wing when she joined the department four years ago. Sometimes it's as if she's five years older than me rather than the reverse. She deals with four other academics, all men, but my gender works in my favour here. She does all sorts of things for me that she would never do for my male colleagues.

Now I've recovered my pencil and myself, I feel able to look Kate in the face. Though I'm very fond of her, I don't want her monitoring all my activities. 'What's the rush?' My blushes have gone but my heartbeat is still too fast.

'I promised him you'd call before your meeting. He said he's going to be away for most of this afternoon.'

'I'll try,' I say. 'Thanks for the message.'

Kate smiles once more. It's as if she knows I want nothing more than to speak to Anthony Blake. After she leaves, I lock the office door. There's not enough time to phone Anthony before the board meeting, I tell myself, and I should read the papers beforehand. But I try picking up the phone, and punching in a few digits of the number Kate has given me: my hands are shaking too much to continue. I put the receiver down, and try experimenting with what I might say when the phone is answered. 'Hello,' I tell my empty room. 'Can I speak to Anthony Blake please?' My voice sounds quite calm, so I try a little more. 'Hello, Anthony. It's Sally Lachlan here.' But my vocal cords have become tense, the words I speak sound strangled. I'm too agitated. I can't do this. It's far worse than standing up in front of a lecture hall of three hundred first-year students doing Introduction to Biology. I can't return a simple phone call from a man I hardly know.

My watch says twelve-twenty. Only forty minutes before the meeting, and it will take ten minutes to get there. I look out the window at the low sky that is the colour of over-washed aluminium.

I've almost forgotten what Anthony looks like. I try to conjure up his image but can't. Sitting at the computer I type in the website address for Imperial College, and after several more clicks retrieve Anthony's picture, there, in the top left-hand corner of his homepage. Once more I have that feeling of recognition. He must remind me of someone, but I can't think who. This photo appears to have been taken some years ago. Anthony's face is three-quarters turned to the viewer and he is smiling, showing white teeth. His hair is darker than when I met him. On the screen his eyes look grey, and not the vivid blue that I remember; grey like the October sky outside.

Idly I examine his features again, as if I have

all the time in the world. Perhaps Anthony is vain; this is a very flattering image. Then I think of my own homepage and how I want to avoid having the college photographer — one of the physics technicians — take a picture of me. Some of my colleagues have had three or four visits to the technician's office before they've been satisfied. The departmental head would have gone in for air brushing if it had been available.

We are none of us perfect.

After shutting down the website, I pick up the phone. Before my hand has time to start shaking, I dial the number Kate gave me. After several rings, there is a click, and more ringing until the phone is picked up by the departmental administrator. No, she informs me, Anthony Blake is not in. He won't be back until tomorrow. I leave her my home number. She has trouble understanding my last name until I spell it out for her. 'Ah, Larcklan,' she says, as if I have mispronounced my own name, 'Sally Larcklan.'

So that is it. I have done it, but I am no further forward. And I shall be late and uninformed for the meeting. It is almost one o'clock.

I have spent half an hour dreaming in front of a computer screen.

12

THEN

Jeff and I had been separated for over six months and I was two years into my PhD before I decided to do some research on domestic violence. 'Battered women,' I typed into the library's search facility. Twenty references appeared on the computer screen, and I scrolled through them quickly. The few survey references seemed the most promising. Two of them were in the college library and the others were in Senate House. I chose the Senate House library because I didn't want to see anyone I knew. This literature search was one to conduct in private. It certainly wasn't part of my thesis on stem cells. I printed out a page with the references and library shelf codes of the books that looked interesting, and stuffed it into my bag.

At Senate House I was lucky: all the books I wanted were where they should have been on the library shelves. This state of affairs wouldn't last long; after term started volumes would go missing, shoved by undergraduate students into remote crannies so that only they could retrieve them. I spread the books on a table next to the sociology stacks. Most of the articles were in a jargon I found unappealing, but at last I found one — the most recent — that I could relate to. I took brief notes.

'Hello, Sally,' said a loud voice with an Italian accent.

Startled, I put my hand over my notes before looking up. Silhouetted against the bright light was my friend Alessandra. Although she was finishing a PhD on sociobiology, it had simply not occurred to me that she might hang out in the sociology section of Senate House library.

'What are you doing here?' She didn't bother to disguise her curiosity. Leaning across me, she read aloud the title of the article in the volume of readings in front of me. '*The social construction of deviance: Experts on battered women.* I didn't know you were into social deviance.'

Bloody hell, do I look like I'm into social deviance? At a loss for polite words, I sat open-mouthed like a student being asked a question in a lecture.

This taciturnity didn't matter with Alessandra. She always had enough words for two and that was one of the things I liked about her. If you didn't want to talk, you could let her words roll over you and sweep you along on a relaxing journey that you could choose to dip in or out of.

'Such an important area. I expect it has some parallels with chimpanzees.' Alessandra's research area was evolutionary biology and feminism. She was prone to draw parallels between human behaviour and that of chimpanzees, an endearing trait that my mother was also inclined to follow but from a vantage point that was less flattering to human beings than Alessandra's.

'I know the woman who wrote this chapter,'

Alessandra added. 'She's one of my supervisors. She's made quite a name for herself.'

I shut the book and looked at the clock on the wall behind Alessandra's head.

'Are you leaving?' she said as I stood up. 'I'll walk with you. I'm taking a class at two o'clock.'

We clattered out of the library, Alessandra chatting all the while. Several people looked at us, their faces puckered with disapproval. One of them shushed but to no avail.

'What was the article about?' Alessandra said when we reached the stairwell.

'It's saying that once a woman admits she's a victim of wife assault, she's viewed as deviant if she stays with her partner.' The article was beginning to really annoy me. That was me, *deviant*.

'Double jeopardy,' Alessandra said as we wound our way down the staircase. 'I can see the logic.' She was puffing a bit now, although that didn't interrupt her flow. 'Society expects still-married people to stay together, in spite of high divorce rates. But it doesn't expect battered wives to stay. So if they don't, they're deviant.'

Alessandra's discussion of this topic at such high volume was making me feel stressed and my heart began to thud. At last we reached the white travertine lobby of Senate House, softly lit by its brass light-fittings.

'Your supervisor knows how to make a point,' I said, as we paused on the pavement outside. 'She reckons that battered women are twice attacked. First by their husbands and then by social workers who say they should have left their husbands.'

'Seems a bit strong,' Alessandra said. 'Social workers are there to provide support not judgements.'

'I suppose they do.' As I peered up at the white tower of Senate House rising into the insipid grey sky, I wondered if this was true.

'Would you like to do lunch next week?' Alessandra said. 'I can tell you all about this latest stuff on genes and feminism.'

'Love to. And I can tell you all about Josh Klemperer's plans to get armies of undergraduates breeding rats that rape and rats that are altruistic, so he can compare their genetic structure.'

She laughed. At first I thought she didn't believe me.

'But I know all about that,' she said, as she waved good-bye.

13

NOW

The streets are crowded with people marching towards the Tube station, but their pace is too slow for someone who has been listening all afternoon to the finer points of the new e-mathematics degree scheme. I weave my way around pedestrians going my direction and avoid eye contact with people coming towards me. This is how to avoid being forced off the footpath; if they think I haven't seen them, they duck away at the last minute, averting disaster.

Once across Euston Road, I steer clear of the main thoroughfares. The side streets are almost completely devoid of people. I stride out towards Regent's Park and on to Primrose Hill, and feel my spirits lifting the further I get from Gower Street.

I take a detour to the top of Primrose Hill and look out across London. To the south, an army of purple and black cumulus clouds is forming, and shortly it begins to march forward, driving in front of it wisps of fluffy grey cloud in panicky retreat. As I watch, the grey sky above turns a bruised yellow and soon this is obliterated by the ranks of advancing black clouds. There is something exciting about the approach of this storm; it's almost as if it might herald a new phase of my life. Exhilarated, I breathe deeply before racing down the hill.

'Spare us some change?' says the emaciated young man standing at the bottom, his hand outstretched. Absent-mindedly I dig in my coat pocket and find a couple of coins to give him. By the time I turn towards home, the sky is completely overcast. The first flash of lightning slices through the dense clouds and a moment later, as I reach our street, I hear the rumble of thunder. By the time I reach our house, fat raindrops are starting to fall.

As I unlock the front door, I smell onions and garlic. I run downstairs to the kitchen and find Charlie making a risotto. She puts out her arms for a hug; I always try to put my arms over her shoulders when we embrace, pretending that I'm still taller than she is, though it has been two years since she overtook me. And then, after a little mock battle that Charlie always wins, I hug her from below.

'There's a message for you on your desk,' she says. 'An Anthony Blake. Quite chatty. He's rung twice. Left his number.'

'He called here?'

'Yeah. Like, I couldn't have spoken to him if he hadn't. He wants you to call back. Said to tell you it's a different number to the one you tried before.'

'Perhaps I'll have a glass of wine first. And Charlie, thanks for doing dinner, you're a darling.'

'Cool, Ma.' Charlie stirs the onions, which are softening in the pan. The salad is on the table already. 'You've got fifteen minutes,' she continues, mimicking the way I speak. 'That'll stop you wittering on and running up the phone bill.'

I pour myself a glass of wine and surreptitiously knock back half in a couple of gulps while Charlie is engrossed in her stirring. When I go up the two flights to my study, I take the glass with me. Charlie has written, on the notepad next to the phone, Anthony's name and number in large block letters. Around the words she's drawn a scalloped border, coloured in with the green fluorescent pen that I keep in the jar on my desk. Around this border she's added some variants of Anthony's name, as she always does with any caller: there is Ant Blake, Tony Baloney, Tone the Drone, and The Blake Bloke. At the bottom of the page she has written in red ballpoint: *Don't be Alone, Phone Tone the Drone!* I transcribe his number to another piece of paper before dialling. After three rings the phone is answered.

'I'm so glad you called back.' Anthony's voice is deeper than I remembered. 'I was starting to wonder if you'd forgotten me.'

'Of course I haven't forgotten you. I really hoped you'd phone me.'

'I tried to call you a couple of times at your office last week but each time the administrator said you were lecturing. I didn't leave a message. I was ringing from Boston and I thought it might be hard for you to return the call. And I tried to send you an e-mail last week but it bounced back.'

'We had problems with our server last week.'

'I'm giving a talk at a conference in Stockholm

on Saturday week. I could stop in London on the way if you're free for dinner on the Friday night. Then I could get the early morning flight to Stockholm the next day.'

'How lovely!' But at that moment I remember the dinner party I'm committed to that evening, given by the head of my department. For one glorious second I imagine taking Anthony with me but dismiss it an instant later. Could I tell the head I'm unable to come after all? Impossible: I like him and his wife and they invited me weeks ago; there's no way I can get out of that dinner without risking offence. Someone on the academic grapevine would be sure to see me with Anthony that same evening. And there's my promotion application coming up; I can't afford to jeopardise this.

After I explain some of this to Anthony, he says, 'Let's do Friday lunch.'

He is easy to talk to on the phone. After a few minutes I feel so relaxed that I lie down on the Balochistan rug and in next to no time Charlie is at the door to tell me the risotto is ready.

'She sounds delightful, your Charlie,' says Anthony. I laugh; evidently Charlie did not try out any of the alternative names for him that she'd written on the margins of her message.

'Who is he?' Charlie says when I return to the kitchen.

'Someone I met at the conference in Spain. He's been at Harvard since then, on leave for the term. He's coming back here again at the end of next week.'

'Cool. What was so urgent?'

'He's asked me out to lunch. On Friday week.'

'Oh,' Charlie says. 'Lunch is not exactly exciting. Or urgent. You often have lunch with people.'

'This is a special lunch, at a special place.' I name a restaurant that even I know is rather fancy, because it's one that Zoë often eats at. 'Such a nice man,' I add, and smile at Charlie.

'A proper man,' Charlie says. 'Like, not a boy.'

'Not a boy,' I repeat slowly, shocked by her remark. Perhaps she meant it as a joke, but it starts me wondering what Zoë has been telling her. I set the table and pour myself another glass of wine.

'He's got loads of gravitas,' Charlie adds; she is trying to make amends by using the expression I often use about some of my more pompous colleagues.

'Gravitas,' I repeat, laughing now. My moment of anxiety has gone. Surely Zoë wouldn't have gossiped to Charlie about my unsuitable past boyfriends.

14

THEN

Jeff was working hard, staying late at the office a couple of nights a week. We no longer had any money worries: his practice was doing well and I was supported by my PhD studentship. One evening in late spring, I decided to surprise him in his office, to take him something nice to eat; a gesture not of love, but of coexistence. I lined up the babysitter and caught the bus into Covent Garden.

Sitting upstairs at the front of the double-decker bus, I watched the crowds of people milling along the streets after work. On my lap was a basket with a picnic in it: smoked salmon and fresh crusty bread, a green salad with the chilli-soaked black olives that Jeff loved, and a bottle of cold dry white wine. I felt such a delightful glow of anticipation, more at the prospect of summer than of surprising Jeff.

There was no one about in Jeff's building, a large terraced house not far from Long Acre. After unlocking the main door, I walked up the stairs to his office. It was on the top floor, and connected to the landing by a wall of plate glass. His office lobby was lit with spotlights and furnished only with a reception desk and a black leather couch. It was like a stage set. All very minimalist.

When I saw the figures on the couch I stopped still. Though I wanted to run back down the stairs again and out into the warm evening, I couldn't move my legs. I was stuck there on the landing, right under one of the down-lights, so that I too would have been fully illuminated. I was shocked at the sight of Jeff on the couch. A woman was straddling him. They were both naked under the blazing spotlights.

Although the woman's face was turned away from me, I knew from the shape of her head that I'd never seen her before. She had a long neck and short platinum blonde hair, and her skin was tanned: I could see the marks from a bikini.

I stood there, frozen on the landing, watching this woman ride my husband hard. And then Jeff looked up at me. He saw me, I swear he did. I will never be able to forget the way he stared at me. Detached, caught up in the act of sex. But triumphant too. He had struck me another blow. He found that exciting, and he found it exciting that I was watching.

And he smiled. He smiled at me not at her. An instant later they both climaxed. She shrieked as she climaxed, this woman, she shrieked. Quite uninhibited, although she didn't know I was there. But Jeff did. He watched me observing him being unfaithful. And he was happy that I'd seen him.

His expression when he saw me shocked me. This and the infidelity left me shaking. It was as if a prop that had been keeping me upright had been removed in a heartbeat, leaving me without any support. Somehow I made my way down the stairs and out of the building. There was a homeless man sitting on a heap of cardboard just down from the bus stop. When I gave him the picnic basket, he mumbled a reply but I couldn't hear the words.

I leaned against the shelter by the bus stop. My legs were trembling still and my stomach beginning to churn. Jeff was fundamentally nasty. Was it the infidelity that bothered me? I didn't think so. If our marriage had been strong, we could have weathered this and stayed together. I'd known for some time that Jeff was capable of physical cruelty and I'd also learned of his mental cruelty. But his smile as he had sex with that woman while I watched had taken this to a new level.

I suppose it was the realisation that he was intrinsically nasty as well as quick-tempered that made it easy to reach a decision. We couldn't carry on together any longer.

★　★　★

The babysitter was surprised when I got home earlier than she'd expected. I could tell she wasn't all that happy to be interrupted in the middle of the DVD she was watching. 'Take it with you,' I said as I fumbled in my purse, and found enough to give her an extra hour's pay. After she'd gone home — she lived with her parents around the corner — I phoned the YWCA and booked a twin room for Charlie and me. I took down two suitcases from the loft, and filled one with my clothes that I pulled at random out of the wardrobe. Only when I was about to close the lid did I remember my laptop with all my files. I put it on top of my clothes and toiletries, and shut the suitcase.

I was becoming more and more anxious: not about what lay ahead but that Jeff might arrive home before I was ready to leave. After collecting some towels and sheets and an armful of Charlie's clothes, I piled these into the second case. Charlie was still asleep when I carried the bags downstairs to the front door. In Jeff's study I found some notepaper and began to write with a hand that shook so much the writing was illegible. I crumpled up the sheet and began to write on another piece of paper in block capitals.

JEFF,
I CAN NO LONGER STAY WITH YOU.
AFTER SEEING YOU TONIGHT I KNEW
IT WAS OVER. I HAVE TAKEN CHARLIE
SOMEWHERE SAFE AND WILL CALL
YOU IN A FEW DAYS' TIME.
SALLY

I put the note on the hallstand where Jeff couldn't fail to see it as soon as he opened the front door. Then I picked up the phone and punched in my parents' number. The answerphone clicked on. I left a message saying that Charlie and I were fine but that we were moving into a hotel for a few nights. My voice cracked and broke altogether, and it was a few seconds before I was able to clear my throat. 'I'll phone you tomorrow morning,' I said before the machine clicked off.

At this moment I heard a car pull up in the crescent. My heart missed a beat. What if Jeff had come home earlier than he usually did on the nights he was supposed to be working late? I shifted the suitcases into the living room, behind the door. I hadn't drawn the curtains yet, although it was already dark. If Jeff saw that I was planning to leave I had a pretty good idea of how he'd react. But peering around the window frame, I saw only Jim Hunter from two doors down, alighting from his car with a carrier bag from the Thai takeaway on Upper Street.

The clock on our mantelpiece showed that it was already gone nine, later than I'd thought. From the kitchen I collected a large shopping bag. Next I called for a taxi before running upstairs to Charlie's room. When I heard a noise from below, I stopped on the landing. Was that the front door clicking open? I stood still. Not a sound until I heard the staircase squeak. Was Jeff home? For a few more seconds I stayed where I was, listening. All I could hear now was the blood thumping in my ears and distant traffic from the high street. That creaking I'd heard must have been the staircase protesting after I'd raced up from the kitchen. But I had to get a move on. We had to be out of here before Jeff returned.

Charlie was asleep, her thumb in her mouth and an arm around her favourite toy, Edward Bear. After sweeping some of her other soft toys and a few books from the shelves into the shopping bag, I removed the bear from Charlie's grasp and put it on top of the books. When I picked up Charlie, she awoke enough to put her arms around my neck. She was heavy and it was a struggle to carry her downstairs, and the bag of toys knocked against my leg at every step. I opened the front door and I saw a taxi parked in front of our house. Heart pounding in my throat, I stopped still. I'd left it too late. Jeff was home and he'd be furious at what I was about to do.

But it wasn't Jeff. The taxi contained only the driver. He saw me and climbed out. As he carried the suitcases from the hall to the cab, I took one last look around. The note was where I'd left it on the hallstand, fully visible. I took a deep breath: this was it, the moment I'd been thinking about for years. The detached but triumphant expression on Jeff's face that I'd seen a couple of hours before returned to me. It made me feel sick but it sharpened my resolve. I didn't ever want to see this house again. Still holding Charlie, I slammed the door shut behind us.

'Where are we going, Mummy?'

'For a ride in the taxi.'

'I've dropped Edward.'

'It's OK, I've got him in the bag.' I put her on the seat and fastened the belt.

'Where are my other toys?'

'They're here, darling, with Edward. And your favourite books are here too.' The driver started the engine and the cab rolled forward.

'Are we going to Grandma and Grandpa's?'

'Not tonight. We're going to stay in a hotel. We're going to have a nice little holiday.'

'Why does your voice sound so funny?'

'Does it? I must have got a bit of dust caught in my throat.'

'I hope you're not getting a cold.'

'So do I, Charlie, so do I.' But catching a cold was the least of my worries.

15

NOW

The clock's luminous dial shows five-forty five and it's Tuesday morning again. I turn on the radio and restlessly roll around the bed, trying to get comfortable; I feel as if my life is being measured out in Tuesday mornings and meetings with Helen. When the duvet slides off the bed, I give up the hard work of trying to sleep and get up. The sound of the radio follows me as I drift down the stairs. 'Genetic engineering is a hit and miss procedure,' a voice calmly explains. 'We have . . . '

By half-past six I am sitting at the computer in my study. As I log on, the date flashes up on the screen: 9 October.

Today is the anniversary of my first meeting with Jeff.

Those early years before we married were the happy times. I haven't thought of them for nearly a decade and yet they sustained me for years.

After working for half an hour, I take the surprised Charlie a cup of coffee before dashing out of the house, barely in time to catch the 7.30 bus to South End Green. I am determined; I am ready to tell Helen about my marriage.

She is wearing her usual long black skirt and a black V-necked sweater that is unmistakably cashmere. Today there are white daisies in the vase on her coffee table. The room smells faintly of their fragrance. I place on the table the envelope I collected last week. It now contains my cheque; I have crossed out my name and scrawled Helen's below it. She gracefully acknowledges the envelope and waves me to the sofa.

I waste no time inspecting my nails or gazing around the room, but at once get on with what I've decided to tell her. I talk continuously, my words like a water-release from an overfilled dam: faster and faster the sentences spill out, until at last I've finished.

I'm unaware of the tears on my face until I see Helen towering over me, with a box of tissues in her hand.

I take a handful of tissues. I wipe my eyes and blow my nose.

And then the floodgates are closed.

There is silence. Feeling strangely detached, I look through the window at the sky. The sun has come out; the first time I've seen it for several weeks. But the patch of blue sky surrounding it is small, and dark clouds are gathering at its edges. A shaft of sunlight streams through the window, fine motes of dust swirling in the ray of light. Even Helen has dust in her beautiful white Hampstead room, with its neat bookshelves and carefully positioned vase of white daisies.

I lift up my hand, the one that once bore Jeff's ring. My vision blurs as I hold it up to the light. The human hand has twenty-seven bones, fourteen of which are the phalanges of the fingers. I turn the hand, a miracle of mobility. At last I've laid out in front of Helen the bare bones of my unhappy marriage, the bits that have lasted while the flesh of the happy times has almost completely rotted away.

Only now do I notice that the box of tissues has appeared somehow on the sofa next to me. I blow my nose again and dry my eyes. Mascara comes off onto the tissue. When it falls onto the floor I'm unable to move to retrieve it. Helen clears her throat. I wait for the words that will follow. She says, 'You've had a terrible time, Sally.'

Again there is silence. I listen to the clock and its relentless tick-tick-tick, the countdown to the end of my session.

Helen coughs, before saying, 'Did you think you deserved it?'

My heart becomes a thumping thing in my throat. I swallow and take a deep breath.

But I don't know how to respond.

'Perhaps you thought you deserved to be punched.' Although Helen's tone is gentle, she articulates each word clearly, as if she thinks I've lapsed into deafness.

Unwillingly I focus my thoughts. Helen deserves a response and there's not much time left. 'No,' I say, quite sure of this.

'Why do you think you stayed with him?'

'I loved him.' Yet I know this is not the whole truth.

'Even though he hit you repeatedly?'

'But I loved him! Can't you understand that?' I'm speaking rather too loudly. At this moment I feel a rush of anger and I channel it at Helen; it's her fault that I'm having to defend myself. 'I loved him,' I repeat, slowly and — in spite of my anger — calmly, to show Helen I am in control of myself. 'He was beautiful and charming when we met.'

'I cannot help wondering how often he hit you.'

'Maybe a dozen times in those first six years.'

'A dozen times.' Helen repeats this slowly, giving each word emphasis. 'That's a lot of times, Sally.'

'Everything is relative,' I say. But I don't intend to be flippant.

I look at the golden patch of sunlight on Helen's white wall. I can hear children playing in the street outside. Although their voices are clear, I can't make out what they are saying.

'I know you don't condone violence against women.' Helen's voice is soft but the words are shards of glass. 'But did it never occur to you that he might physically abuse Charlie as well?'

'Never. That was another reason I stayed; I wanted Charlie to have a proper live-in father.'

'Even a violent one,' Helen murmurs so quietly that I can barely catch her words. When they sink in, I'm enraged by their implication.

'I could do nothing. I could do nothing!' I am shouting at her now, and hot tears are filling my eyes.

There is a pause before Helen continues. 'Perhaps it was hard for you accept any failure.' Her voice is as calm as if we are talking of the weather. 'Academics are often perfectionists.'

I feel as if she has punched me and lie very

still. After a few seconds I start inhaling deeply, calming myself with each daisy-scented intake. In and out, in and out, my chest rises and falls with the mechanical action of breathing.

It is possible that Helen has a point. A perfectionist; I am certainly that.

'Jeff never hit Charlie,' I say, wiping my eyes with a sodden tissue. 'Never, ever, did he do that.'

'He didn't hit you to begin with, Sally.'

'Are you suggesting I should have left him, or that I should have fought him? That it was somehow my fault that I allowed him to continue?'

Helen doesn't reply. The patch of sunlight is moving along the wall, and there is a small fly buzzing outside the top sash of the window. My hour is nearly over. I paraphrase to myself the lines from a poem by John Donne that I haven't thought of for years: I am two fools, I know, for marrying and for staying so.

But in fact I'm three fools for paying to talk to Helen about this. 'So you think I'm a fool because I married Jeff, and I'm a fool because I stayed married to him.' I can't keep the bitterness out of my voice.

I hear her crossing her legs and the sound of her pencil on the pad she keeps by her. She is making a note of my cynicism.

'What have you got to say about that?' We both know my question is rhetorical.

'I'm afraid we'll have to stop there,' she says. 'Till next Tuesday, Sally.'

She ushers me out of the room, and lightly

touches my shoulder as I pass. It's the first time she's ever done this.

I stumble down the stairs, blowing my nose on a dry tissue I find in my pocket. Before opening the front door, I dig my dark glasses out of my bag and put them on.

The sky is now grey, except for one patch of blue in which the sun is corralled. Slowly I walk along the pavement until I am out of sight of Helen's house, and there I sit on someone's brick fence.

It is over. My marriage is over. It's been over for more than ten years.

When I stand up, I step on something soft. My tread releases the stench of dog turd. I lift my foot to examine the sole of my shoe; a sticky yellow mess is caught in the fine corrugations. Too many dogs in London shitting everywhere. I scrape the mess off on a pile of dead leaves caught up against a low brick wall. The smell is overpowering and I feel sickened; sickened by the excrement, sickened at the thought of Jeff.

16

THEN

On the day my mother phoned to let me know that Celia had died, she didn't bother with any introductory remarks, not even to say hello. In a matter-of-fact voice, she said that Celia had passed away the previous night, peacefully in her sleep.

I sat down cross-legged on the polished floor in the living room of Jeff's and my house in Islington. Although it was a relief to know that Celia wouldn't have a painfully drawn out end, her death still seemed shocking. No more chats with her. No more thinking of snippets to tell her as I drove out to Buckinghamshire. Her death meant the end of an era as well as a reminder of my own mortality. I thought of that express train rushing us all to eternity. The one that we could never get off.

My mother began to tell me of Celia's wishes, that she wanted her ashes to be scattered in the sea off St Mawes on the south coast of Cornwall, where Celia's husband had been harbour master. Thirty years before, his ashes had been strewn outside the harbour and Celia wanted to join him. My mother spoke about the ashes with heavy irony, as if she were discussing the cricket series with Australia, and she laughed. But I knew she was upset; she had adored Celia.

Although she was calm at first, soon the tears came. When Charlie and I turned up at my parents' place later that day, my mother's eyes were red-rimmed and swollen. Charlie hugged my mother and earnestly explained to her that I was upset too, even though I hadn't been crying. That made my mother laugh; Charlie has always been able to do that.

Two weeks after Celia's death was the earliest time that we were all able to get together in Cornwall to cast her ashes to the sea. It was an imaginative gesture, I thought, and a lovely way to celebrate her life.

That day marked a turning point for me and not only because I'd loved Celia. Towards noon we all climbed on board the harbour master's boat, a small launch that was still referred to as a cutter although it relied on a diesel motor rather than wind power. Thirty years of movements of the tides, and the silt and rubbish lining the bottom of the harbour, made it highly unlikely that Celia would be reunited with her husband. His ashes were probably thousands of miles away by now. But the ceremony proceeded, in a way that seemed slightly surreal.

We were dressed in a sober manner in dark suits, looking incongruous in the setting. My father gingerly held a small clear plastic bag, through which the earthly remains of Celia were visible. She may not have wished to be so exposed to the general view. I'd expected that something more substantial would contain the ashes: a small wooden cask perhaps, or a ceramic urn.

It was a beautiful day, the sky a pale clear blue although the water was choppy. As we puttered out from the shelter of St Mawes harbour and into the main part of the river, the rocking of the boat increased. The harbour master tried to hold it stationary in the face of the heavy swell. Jeff lifted his face up to the sun: hedonistically he basked in it, almost as if he were on a pleasure cruise. I sat next to my father, who'd been discussing with the harbour master the whiteness of the ashes in the plastic bag. They looked like small marble chips, and I wondered if they had been bleached or otherwise treated between their immersion in fire and their imminent immersion in water. So little remained. It was hard to believe that the contents of that little bag were all that was left of Celia.

My father cleared his throat. He said a few words, but they were lifted and tossed towards the shore by the breeze, so that we had only a vague idea of what he was saying. Celia and her husband, it appeared, would be reunited both beneath the seas and in heaven. His speech finished, my father wrestled with the plastic bag. Its top had been heat-sealed. No one had thought to bring scissors. The harbour master found a ballpoint pen in the inside pocket of his jacket, and handed it to my father, who used it to puncture the plastic. After widening the hole with his large awkward fingers, he pushed his hand further into the bag, and ran the ashes through his fingers. Quickly he withdrew his hand and wiped it surreptitiously on his trouser leg. An instant later, he leaned over the side of the boat to launch his cargo to eternity. Clutching at the gunwale with one hand, he flicked the bottom of the plastic bag several times with the other. The flapping back of his jacket emphasised the precariousness of the operation. The white ashes poured out and were blown beyond the range of the boat.

The flakes floated momentarily on the surface of the water, before they were caught up in the momentum of the waves and swirled towards our craft. The harbour master flicked the engine into reverse. The boat lurched away from its mortuary position and turned towards the harbour at St Mawes. I looked back at the remains of Celia; the ashes were sinking and, a minute later, were gone. Celia had now departed and all that remained of her were our memories.

At that moment I came to a decision. For a while I'd been sitting on an offer of a PhD studentship at University College. Only Celia knew about it. The words she'd spoken to me, on the last day I'd seen her only a month before, returned to me so clearly she might have been right next to me: 'Take it. Don't always do what other people expect of you. *Especially Jeff.*'

I hadn't told anyone else about it, not even Jeff. I'd wanted to make up my own mind first, without being influenced by anyone. What else had she said to me that last time we spoke? Something about needing to protect myself, as well as others.

Of course I would accept the offer. I had to change my life. I didn't want to disappear under the waves — in twenty, thirty, fifty years' time

— having made nothing of myself. So I told my family that day, over lunch, that I was going take up the studentship.

Jeff was pleased. He was pleased even though I'd been sitting on the offer for a while before telling him. Perhaps he didn't realise I'd wanted to make up my mind first and to reveal it only when I had my family in a protective ring around me. And I'd only made the final decision when we were out on the water. Anyway, he seemed thrilled. He knew it would mean more money in the future. I hadn't been able to find a decent job and he could see that having a postgraduate qualification would make me more marketable. And Charlie was already at school. We didn't plan to have any more children. We both thought Charlie was enough.

I remembered still the sweet feel of a baby's downy head against my face, my lips. The milky smells, that fine, smooth skin. But I knew I couldn't bring another child into the world. Not with a man like Jeff.

17

NOW

There is no one in the women's room. A feeble shaft of sunlight struggles through the grimy window. For barely a second, before being obliterated by clouds, it illuminates my face and that of my doppelganger in the mirror above the washbasin. I switch on the fluorescent light and check my hair, which I washed this morning. Exuberant is the word to describe it. Too exuberant; I try flattening it with my hands. While I'm applying some lip liner and lipstick, Kate bursts in. The lipstick is a light brownish shade and barely noticeable.

'Lipstick,' comments Kate at once. 'You don't normally wear it.'

'I'm going out for lunch.'

'You're all dressed up too. Is that a new outfit?'

'No, not really.'

In fact it's Zoë's suit. I phoned her last night to tell her about Anthony's visit and, with her usual kindness, she was at my front door with one of her designer suits within half an hour. She is taller than I am, about the same height as Charlie, but the suit has a short skirt and it fits me well. It's wonderful to wear; the fabric is so light and soft that it feels like a second skin.

'You look lovely,' Kate says. 'A bit of a change

from the old trousers, eh?'

I wipe off the lipstick that I have so carefully applied. Afterwards I decide I looked better with it on, and start to reapply it.

'It suits you, Sally. Don't rub it off again. Where are you going for lunch?'

'Guillaume's.'

'Well, well. Rather special. And expensive too, so I've heard.' Kate is powdering her already flawless skin, standing back to admire the effect. 'Are you doing another book?'

'No academic publisher would take me for lunch there. I'm just meeting a friend.'

'I hope he's paying.'

'So do I.' At once I realise how neatly I've fallen into her trap. In her oblique way she can find out all sorts of things.

She widens her mouth into a broad smile, and expertly applies bright red lipstick. 'You must come to the surprise party I'm organising for Jim,' she says. Her husband is about to turn forty. 'It's in a few weeks' time. You can't possibly be engaged that far ahead! It's on a Saturday afternoon and I've booked a boat for a cruise along the Grand Union Canal. Only through London, but it should be fun. Perhaps you might like to bring someone?'

'Lovely, thanks.' I scribble the date onto one of the scraps of paper in my bag and at that instant remember Kate's stepson, Ben. 'Could I bring Charlie?' I say. Normally Charlie would be reluctant to spend a Saturday afternoon with a bunch of my middle-aged friends. But not so long ago, when Kate and Jim brought Ben to one of my Sunday lunch parties, I noticed how well Charlie and Ben had got along.

'Of course. Ben would love that. By the way,' Kate asks as I'm leaving. 'Your lunch date. Is it with that Professor Blake?'

I pretend not to hear her as the door swings shut behind me.

18

THEN

The night it happened, I couldn't sleep. I tossed and turned in bed for what seemed like hours. My jaw was throbbing. When I got up to go to the bathroom, I could see that my left cheek was swollen from the jawline to the cheekbone. A bruise was developing and it would be a big one.

I went downstairs and sat in the living room. My green and white striped shirt was lying crumpled on the floor. The shirt was my favourite but it was going in the bin.

I began to feel dizzy and stretched out on the couch. What had happened to our love; what was happening to our marriage? I'd been a somebody once, a woman with a bright future. Now I was a nothing. A nobody who didn't have the strength to do anything, let alone leave.

The room was swimming. I felt as if our house was being sliced vertically through the middle, like a doll's house. I could see Charlie sound asleep in her bedroom, dreaming sweetly in a world uncomplicated by responsibilities. And in our bedroom, I could see Jeff sound asleep too, elegant as always, even when he had completely abandoned consciousness. And then I saw myself, there on a couch in the living room, separated from my husband by a couple of solid brick walls and the thickness of the floor.

I felt that I inhabited a different world now.

Yet I was connected to my family by the ties of our common existence in that house. And as I watched, these took tangible form, like some spider's web trapping us as if we were flies. And the threads of the web grew stronger as I watched, and thickened into filaments. It was as if some dreadful fungus, some ghastly growth like dry rot, had taken over our lives, and was catching us up in the fast-growing fibres of its obscene expansion. At that moment, I wondered if I was about to have a nervous breakdown.

But after a while the hallucination slipped away, and I went upstairs and fell asleep. And the following day we carried on as usual, as if nothing had happened to change things between us.

Charlie noticed of course. The next morning I woke up to the pad of her feet across the bedroom floor, the usual early morning occurrence that meant there was no need for an alarm clock. I opened my eyes and looked at her face a few centimetres away; she was kneeling next to the bed watching me.

'What happened, Mummy?' Her voice was a whisper.

'Morning, darling.' I rolled onto my back. Jeff was lying on his side, with his back towards me, still asleep.

'What happened to your face?' Charlie touched my jaw, which felt painful to her touch.

'I walked into a cupboard door. Silly me, I didn't have the light on and couldn't see where I was going.'

'Poor Mummy.'

She climbed onto the bed, and clambered over me into the space next to Jeff. As she snuggled up to me, she gave my shoulder gentle pats, as if I were some fragile thing that she didn't want to see hurt. I pulled her close and curved my body around hers. More and more she was becoming the one I was living for. She felt warm and soft and giving, and she needed my love as much as I needed hers.

When Jeff woke up, he started playing with Charlie as if nothing had happened the previous night. As if nothing had happened.

I put make-up over my bruised jaw and kept a low profile for the following week. If anyone enquired, I said I'd collided with an open cupboard door in the kitchen. As the days slipped by, I felt I was a nothing still. I felt as if my energy was draining away. I had only enough to look after Charlie, and to read again and again the letter from University College offering me a post-graduate studentship.

19

NOW

Although it's raining, the pavement outside the Darwin Building is thronging with lunchtime crowds. The wind blows the rain up under my umbrella and threatens to turn it inside out. I begin to wish that I'd worn a mackintosh over Zoë's suit, the skirt of which is getting splashed. In my unsuitable high-heeled shoes I tip-tap around the piles of leaves and rubbish flitting hither and thither, driven by a wind that cannot make up its mind from which direction it's blowing. In Bedford Square, a few hardy stalwarts are sitting on the benches overlooking the gardens. Huddled under umbrellas, they eat their sandwiches while they fight off the pigeons.

The blustery weather exacerbates my nervousness. When the prospect of seeing Anthony was in the future, I'd been looking forward to it; but the closer I get to my destination the more anxious I become. Perhaps we won't recognise each other; or maybe I've been mistaken about him and we'll have nothing to say.

There is a rumour circulating that he's been offered an endowed professorship at Columbia University in New York. Yesterday afternoon I heard several colleagues discussing this in the common room and one even claimed to know the precise amount of the offer. Ever since, I've been wondering if there's any truth in it. Academics are notorious gossips and although it's possible that an offer has been made, I have no idea if it's likely that Anthony will accept.

By the time I reach Adeline Place, I'm starting to wish I hadn't agreed to this lunch. I look at my watch. I am far too early: fifteen minutes to go and I'm nearly there. To fill in time, I start a second circuit of the square. Three or four joggers straggle past, their joyless expressions revealing a dogged determination to achieve physical fitness regardless of its cost. An old man is lying on a bench; he is covered with a coarse piece of sacking over which is spread a clear plastic sheet, formed from a builders' merchant bag. As I walk by, I catch a whiff of whisky overlaid with urine. I look more closely to see if he is dead, but his chest is rising and falling. I glance at my watch again: ten minutes to go, and it will take only five to reach the restaurant.

At this moment I hear someone call my name and look around, half expecting to see another Sally being hailed. But it's Anthony shouting at me and my pulse rate quickens. He is hurrying towards me from Bayley Street on the west side of the square. His cream raincoat flaps as he runs, revealing a green polo-neck jumper. He stops a metre away, and we look at each other. His hair is almost dripping wet; he has no umbrella. Then he raises his arms and takes hold of my shoulders.

'Wonderful to see you,' he says. He leans under my umbrella, and kisses me on each cheek. 'Serendipity. Now neither of us will have to wait for the other at the restaurant.'

He beams at me, while maintaining his hold on my shoulders. He is close enough for me to see that the skin under his eyes is criss-crossed with fine lines that I find curiously affecting. He tells me he has come from a meeting at Senate House but I don't really take in the detail of what he is saying. I am so pleased to see him that I can't stop smiling. His hair has been darkened by the rain to almost black, against which the few white hairs stand out sharply.

'You're all wet,' I say at last. His eyes look a deeper blue than I remembered; it's as if the grey day has absorbed some of their colour.

'Say that again.'

'You're all wet.'

'No, just say my name.'

'Anthony.'

'I love the way you pronounce it. You put all the emphasis on the first syllable.'

I laugh. 'You've been listening to too many American accents. But your hair really is wet. You're saturated.' And I think back to the other occasion when he stood dripping in front of me, and I had almost caressed his face, in the hotel lobby in Vigo nearly three weeks ago. 'Get under my umbrella. It's big enough for two.'

The enforced closeness of sharing an umbrella is one way of bringing together two reserved people. Anthony takes my umbrella and I take his proffered arm, and we proceed towards the restaurant. With part of my brain I think of the blood pulsing through his cardiovascular system barely millimetres from my own. With a different part of my brain I think of the miracle of two people meeting in central London when yesterday we were thousands of miles apart. But soon I forget to be analytical as he begins to talk. We have no trouble thinking of what to say: it's as if all the face-to-face conversation we might have had over the past few weeks has been dammed up. Released now, it rushes forth in a torrent.

At the restaurant we are shown to a quiet table for two, in front of a stained-glass window. I sit facing the room and Anthony sits opposite. I watch him obliquely while he studies the menu. The light from the window washes over his face: pale lozenges of blue and yellow and mauve, dappled with the faintest shadow of what must be raindrops sliding down the outside of the window behind me.

'Do you remember when we last saw each other in Spain?' he says when we have placed our orders and the waiter has gone.

'Yes, on the terrace.' I don't tell him how often this has been on my mind.

'I really wanted to see you again. I thought Thanksgiving was too long to wait. So when this trip came up, it seemed like an excellent opportunity.'

'Killing two birds with one stone.'

'Well, that's one way of looking at it.' He smiles. 'But you knew we would see each other again soon.' This is a statement and not a question.

'The funny thing is that the day you called I'd more or less decided to send you an e-mail. I was

105

starting to forget what you looked like!'

The waiter brings the main course. After he has gone away, we gossip about colleagues and academic intrigues: who has got an offer from a prestigious US laboratory, who is thinking of moving to Cambridge. This moment would be the ideal time to ask him if there is any truth in the story that he is considering staying in the States. I know I should do this but my mouth refuses to articulate the words. Can I really expect him to reveal his career plans to me, a near stranger? And even if I am more to him than that, can I expect him to reveal his career plans to me, a possible lover? Of course I can. I try to put myself in his position: brilliant scientist, middle-aged bachelor, not bad-looking. Which would come first, the career or the potential love life? The career obviously. That is why he is what he is. And there are plenty of unattached women in the US, plenty of other possibilities.

'What are you thinking about, Sally? You look miles away.'

Apologising, I decide to take a risk even though I mightn't like the answer. 'And you,' I say, choosing my words so carefully that my sentence comes out as if I'm speaking to someone whose first language isn't English. 'And you — are you thinking of staying in North America?'

'Almost certainly not. I like it better here.' Although Anthony's face is impassive, he looks me straight in the eye.

I gaze back while considering his response. I estimate that there is about a five per cent probability he will stay in the States, give or take a bit. It's definitely worth gambling at those odds. I wonder if he can see the relief in my eyes or if instead I look as inscrutable as he does.

We are interrupted by the waiter removing our plates. Anthony asks me about Charlie and I tell him in some detail about her A-levels and how lucky I am having a daughter who causes me little worry. Then I remember I told him this on the way to Spain; perhaps I am too much the doting mother. I also notice that I've finished my second glass of wine. So I stop myself talking and there's a pause in the conversation. Although this might have been the time to do it, Anthony doesn't ask about Charlie's father. So I tell him I am a widow.

'I'm sorry.' He looks quite shocked. He must have thought I was divorced or never married.

'Thank you,' I say automatically. 'My husband Jeff died ten years ago.'

'Do you want to tell me about it?'

'No.' My response is like a slap in the face. I feel ashamed of my abruptness; a flush of heat moves from the base of my neck and slowly ascends to my cheeks.

Anthony raises his eyes to examine the stained glass in the window behind my head. The feeling of intimacy has vanished. I have hurt him and he can't quite hide it. Should I apologise? The thought of telling him about Jeff fills me with dread. Perhaps Anthony thinks I'm still in love with my husband; or maybe only that I've been rude. I can't second-guess him on this. One of the things I've realised since starting my sessions with Helen is that my empathy is the projection of my feelings and reactions on to someone else.

'I'm sorry,' I say. 'That was a bit abrupt. What I really meant to say was, not yet.' Why do I think I have to discuss this with Helen first? I'm starting to feel confused, crippled with indecision. But Anthony is reaching out to touch my hand as it fiddles with the stem of the wine glass. His skin is warm and his touch gentle. Calmed by his gesture, I smile and ask him if he has ever been married.

'No.' He retrieves his hand and begins to play with a fork.

I look away, fearing my need for him will be obvious. I'm not yet ready to risk exposure.

He says, 'I lived with someone when I was in my early thirties and we thought about it.'

I had expected that he would have a serious relationship behind him. He is too pleasant not to have, even though, like all serious academics, his work is probably his main interest.

'But Katherine became ill.' He pauses and inspects the tablecloth; he sweeps some stray breadcrumbs into a neat pile. 'She developed breast cancer. It was a particularly virulent kind that had spread before it was discovered. She was dead within six months.' He is speaking quickly. Unlike me, he is glad of this opportunity to unburden himself.

'How terrible. You must have had an awful time.'

Now he is focusing on the single white rose in a vase in the centre of our table. Although its petals are tightly furled, they are already beginning to wither at the edges.

How grim those six months must have been. Perhaps his reaction to my widowhood was a shock of recognition; he might think we have a similar past. I reflect on the statistics — the one-in-twelve chance women face of dying from breast cancer — while I watch Anthony contemplating the white rose. His face is set and tense. He is probably still not over his loss; he may never recover from his loss.

'She died five years ago.' He glances up at me for an instant before resuming his rearrangement of the pile of breadcrumbs on the cloth in front of him. He tells me about the guilt he felt, as if Katherine's cancer were somehow his fault, especially once he discovered that her grandmother had also had breast cancer. 'We should have been on the lookout for it,' he says. 'I'm a geneticist but I didn't even have the wit to consider how genetics might affect the woman I was going to marry.' He has stopped playing with the crumbs and is now engaged in rearranging the salt and pepper.

'You can't blame yourself.'

When he raises his eyes to meet mine they are no longer shuttered and for a brief instant, I see his pain. Then he banishes all emotion and his face becomes a blank, but I know he wouldn't be here if he really wanted to shut me out. An insidious little thought creeps unbidden into my mind; that it's because of Katherine's bad luck that I am sitting in a Soho restaurant with her partner and looking with hope towards the future.

'I'm so sorry,' I say, both for his anguish and

for my thought. 'It must be a terrible thing to see someone you love in pain.' My words seem inept but I can't think of a better way to express sympathy. I try to imagine what it would be like to lose Charlie. Impossible; I would go mad with grief. 'And to lose Katherine so young,' I continue. 'It must have seemed so unfair.'

Anthony doesn't seem to want to say any more and we sit in silence. I take a sip of wine and try to think of how to turn the conversation around. At the next table, three men dressed in almost identical dark suits appear to be discussing the plot of a play, but after a couple of seconds it becomes clear it's the outline of a TV commercial. Two of the men are wearing T-shirts under their suit jackets, in a subtle differentiation of the usual male uniform. Both of the T-shirts are black.

All the tables are occupied. If we could speed up time, we would see people coming and going, moving in, moving out, dancing through their days, through their lives. Anthony and I are together today but in the past we have overlapped with countless other people: acquaintances, friends, parents, lovers like Katherine and Jeff. We are like two arcs intersecting. Perhaps we shall travel the same trajectory for a while.

'I've had a few affairs since Katherine died,' Anthony says at last, interrupting my reverie. 'But nothing serious. So to answer your question, no, I've never been married.'

He appears intent to the point of single-mindedness on being honest about his past and I feel touched by his directness. Although I wonder what he means by 'a few' affairs, that's not something that I wish to ask him. And I certainly don't want to be caught up in confidences about the young men I dated. Some things are best kept concealed.

Lunch is over. The waiter is hovering restlessly nearby and the restaurant is starting to empty. Anthony insists on paying on the grounds that it was his idea to eat at an expensive place. While we wait for the return of his credit card, I tell him about my recent visit to the Tate Modern. On an impulse, I ask if he'd like to go there with me now. He agrees at once; he hasn't been for a while. If we take a cab we can have an hour or two there before I head off to the dinner with my departmental head and his wife, and Anthony visits his parents in Golders Green.

How can the promise of a couple of extra hours bring so much happiness?

20

NOW

Although it is still drizzling outside, the wind has dropped. In spite of the rain, we immediately secure a taxi. I sit by the window; Anthony leaps in after me and sits in the middle of the bench seat. Blackfriars Bridge looms in sight, gaudily painted red and white, a relief from the drab grey of the London streets. I don't need to look down to know that Anthony's elbow is barely a centimetre away from my arm.

The cab corners suddenly and we are thrown against each other. The shock is electric. Abruptly we move apart, the action unnatural; it's as if we have both become negatively charged, two opposing forces pushing each other away. All it will take is a quick flick of the switch and we'll be pulled together once more.

The consciousness of Anthony's body so close to mine heightens my powers of observation, as if I need to commit to memory not only every detail of Anthony but every detail of our environment too. I see, beyond his profile, a train stopped at the station that spans a part of the river. A blue and white sign says: WELCOME TO LONDON BLACKFRIARS. People are scurrying along the platform towards the exit, their shoulders hunched against the rain and the leaden grey sky pressing down like a lid over

London. The River Thames, muddy as always, flows fast with the out-going tide, and undulates around the buttresses of the bridge.

Anthony speaks my name. On its own: no embellishments. The way he says this word is so powerful that I hear it with my whole body. I tingle all over, as if I've just stepped out of the coldest water and onto a warm beach.

Shocked, I remain silent. And perhaps there is no need to respond. Everything was there in the way he said my name. We sit side-by-side looking out of the cab windows. I barely notice that Tate Modern is now in sight, a squat oblong like a shoebox, redeemed from ugliness by its bold chimney and the strong flutings of its brickwork.

The cab driver puts us down on the south side of the bridge next to the greengrocer whose stall is set up under an awning on the pavement. It's raining very lightly still. I put up my umbrella but Anthony takes it from me. Threading my arm through his, I feel the warmth of his body. It is one thing to feel desire but this need, which hits me like a tidal wave, has struck without warning.

We walk down the steps to the Thames and through the tunnel of yellow brickwork whose flying buttresses and vaults support the railway above us. A few gulls are wheeling low over the river, and a passing tug hoots softly. Whatever happens, I will always remember this moment, and this view that is like a tapestry. A beautiful tapestry of muted colours, through which our happiness is being woven, thread by golden thread.

Tate Modern, when we can see it again after passing the housing on our right, no longer looks squat, but is a powerful statement. Its vast load of brickwork presses down onto two narrow horizontal slits at ground level that look as if they are waiting for some enormous letters to be posted.

I take Anthony up to the galleries on level three, which I think he will find the most interesting. He is fascinated by a Tinguely construction, a large machine that is sitting idly on the gallery floor. While we stand there, an attendant appears and starts it up; he operates it for five minutes every hour, he explains. Our small group expands almost at once to a fascinated crowd of forty or more. We watch mesmerised as the machine pursues its useless actions, cogs and wheels operating, setting off other cogs and wheels, a great machine working purposefully at producing nothing.

'Like the academic world,' I say.

'You cynic. We do make some breakthroughs. You're one of those who do.'

'I know all that stuff about building on the shoulders of giants.'

'Maybe it's a model of the funding councils.' Anthony steps back slightly as a man pushes in front of us and obliterates our view of the sculpture. 'A button's pressed somewhere, in some government department. Then the funding council moves into action, cogs turn, wheels spin, new organisations are spawned. But none of them actually produces anything.'

'Now who's being cynical!'

We move on to look at a painting close by that I missed on my previous visit. Books are glued onto its surface, with their covers backing onto the canvas so that the pages of the books fan out. Spread-eagled open to the viewer, the pages have been crudely painted in a variety of colours, and sculpted into curves. The artist made a film of the canvas, Anthony reads from the placard on the wall. The artist first photographed one arrangement of the pages, and afterwards turned over a few leaves of every book before taking another photograph. In repeating the process, he created a moving film of the pages flipping over on his canvas.

'Read the book and see the film,' says Anthony. 'It's a neat concept.'

I squint at the canvas to comprehend it better. It's like someone's life, each page so detailed, so complex. But speed up the turning of each sheet and you're left with just a blur, and then it's all over. Better by far to see the canvas as it is, static. You can take your pick about which page to focus on. You can take one day at a time. Like today; take it slowly. Savour it while it's here.

'I like it static,' I say softly, not wanting to explain why. 'It looks so organic, like a banksia cone.'

He looks at me blankly; it can't be often that he doesn't know something.

'You're a biologist,' I tell him, smiling. 'You should know all about banksias. They're an Australian shrub with the most wonderful gnarled cones.'

He laughs. 'I never did any botany.'

115

The Tinguely sculpture nearby has ceased operating, and the little crowd of onlookers begins to disperse, some of them heading our way. I look at my watch. The gallery will close in half an hour. We move off; I want Anthony to see Rothko's Seagram series of paintings, my favourites in this gallery.

Anthony seizes my hand, and the physical shock of this takes my breath away. His hand is large and warm, and infinitely comforting. In a daze I lead him along a corridor to the gallery exhibiting Rothko's large red canvases. This space has been made deliberately dark. Anthony and I sit on a bench. The room is practically empty; there is only one other couple that is keeping their distance.

In silence we contemplate the painting on the wall opposite. It is of two reddish-lavender vertical rectangles; they are bounded by fuzzy-edged black scaffolding on a deep maroon background. Intensely aware of Anthony, I can feel the blood pumping through his hand. After a while the painting begins to take the form of an invitation. Do step in, it is saying. Do step right in, right into the canvas, right into this brave new world I am offering you.

'Here's to our friendship,' Anthony says at last, as if he too is affected by what we're seeing together.

'May it last.'

He turns to me, his expression surprised. 'Why shouldn't it?'

'We don't know each other at all,' I say, while thinking that we have so far not arranged when to meet again. And he doesn't know of my past yet either.

'Well, we're going to remedy that,' he says quite firmly. 'I'm coming back again at Thanksgiving and I hope we can see a lot of each other then. And I think I'll start phoning you at regular intervals too, just to make sure you don't forget me.'

'Not much chance of that.'

He laughs. As we come out of the darkened room into the adjacent space, we catch a glimpse of the rows of silver birches defining the edge of the Thames. Outside the sun has emerged from its grey shroud and is shining on the dome of Saint Paul's Cathedral. The gilded cross on its top blazes with light.

Anthony hails a passing cab and I climb in. He leans forward and kisses me. It is a gentle touch but one that lingers on my lips and promises more. 'I wish you weren't leaving so soon,' I say.

'I'll see you in four weeks. But I'll phone you early next week when I'm back at Harvard.' And with a wave he has gone.

Raising my fingertips to my lips, I feel charged with new energy. Four weeks will fly by. The taxi drops me at Gower Street, and I bounce into the college building. I am walking on air, I am weightless.

Only later, during the dinner party that evening with my departmental head and his wife, does a subversive little thought return to me. It is the same thought that sprang into my head the night I first told Zoë about meeting Anthony. That maybe he is just too perfect.

21

THEN

I put Charlie to bed soon after we got home from seeing Jeff's prospective clients, the Fosters, and came downstairs again. I said, 'They haven't phoned yet, Jeff?'

Mr Foster had said he'd ring that night if Jeff had the job of doing the landscape design for his new development.

'No.' Jeff put down his newspaper and looked at me. I was wearing my outdoor jacket over my green and white striped shirt and black jeans. 'Why have you changed?'

'The dress was a bit uncomfortable.'

'Where are you going?'

'To the shop.'

'What do we need?'

'More milk. Charlie drank the last of it before she went to bed.'

'Surely it can wait till tomorrow.'

'I feel like some fresh air.' I gave him a quick kiss and was out the front door in a flash. I never could bear hanging around when Jeff was waiting for a phone call. He was always so irritable.

I walked up our crescent and on through the dark deserted streets of Islington. Although I felt moderately confident Jeff would get that job, I knew that he'd be in a foul temper if he didn't.

Earlier he'd told me I'd behaved badly at the

Fosters. Charlie had been tired when we arrived there and, as always when she was tired and placed in a new environment, she became hyperactive. 'Control her, why can't you,' he whispered when the Fosters had left us alone in their living room for a moment.

Charlie at once escaped from my grasp and dashed into the hallway. I could hear her pounding up and down the stairs. Mrs Foster caught me charging after her. 'Lovely child,' she said. 'Kids always love the stairs.' She had one of those faces that seemed to be perpetually smiling, as if everything you said was a joke. 'We have three sons, all grown up. So we're used to children.'

'She's normally not as bad as this.'

'She's fine, Sally. Don't you worry about her.' I liked Mrs Foster for that and liked her even more when she put her arm around Charlie and said, 'Come and I'll show you something. It's a wooden train set. I know you're going to really love playing with it. My boys certainly did. I'm keeping it for my grandchildren, if I'm lucky enough to have any.'

On the way home afterwards, Jeff criticised me for not controlling Charlie properly. 'You didn't make enough conversation either. Half the battle in private practice is charming the client,' he said.

Now, in the dark Islington street that was lit only by a few sodium lamps, I tripped on a half-empty lager can that someone had left on the footpath and beer sloshed on my ankle. At the pedestrian crossing beyond the supermarket in Upper Street, I saw a frail stooped woman in a long black coat waiting at the lights. Her dried-up brown face wore the appearance of a small child looking with wonder at the world. Earlier that afternoon I'd seen a similar expression when I'd waved goodbye to poor old Celia, who was living out her remaining days in the residential care home. My vision blurred but I saw the lights change colour. The woman picked up her torn plastic holdall and struggled across the road. That would be me in forty years' time. Sooner probably.

After buying the milk, I trudged home. It began to rain, quite heavily, just as I left Upper Street. I hadn't thought to bring an umbrella; the rain trickled down my face and into the gap between collar and neck. When I turned into our crescent, I heard a phone start to ring. Surely that must be ours. I slowed my pace, but no, it was from the house next door but one. As I reached our place I heard a new peal. I hesitated outside the front door until the ringing stopped and then I inserted my key into the lock. It was probably the Fosters. They would surely not be calling unless Jeff had got the job.

Jeff wasn't in the living room. The house was quiet; he must have already finished talking on the phone, or perhaps he was on the extension in our bedroom upstairs. I hoped he wasn't going to wake Charlie. I crept up the stairs and still I could hear nothing. But the bathroom light was on: a band of light shone from under the closed door and Jeff came out as I got to the top of the stairs.

'Did you get it?' I asked.

'Get what?'

'The job. Wasn't that the Fosters on the phone?'

'I don't know. I didn't answer it. Why the hell didn't you pick it up?'

'I've only just got home.'

'I thought you were back already. Wasn't there a message?'

'I didn't check. But they'll call you back. You know they will.' I smiled and reached out to touch his arm.

'Don't you treat me like a child!' His voice was too quiet and I grew cold with apprehension.

An instant later he punched me hard in the jaw.

And the phone started ringing again.

I ran into the bathroom, and shut the door quietly behind me. My left cheek felt numb. I knew it was the shock. I ran my tongue carefully over my teeth. Nothing was broken. My face in the mirror was stark white, with a blazing red mark where Jeff's fist had hit me. Still I felt nothing. No physical pain. No emotional pain. Nothing, just nothing. No anger. No hurt.

I felt nothing at all.

I was nothing.

I sat down on the floor between the bath and basin, with my back against the cold wall tiles, and put my forehead on my knees.

I waited for something to happen. For some reaction.

But still I felt nothing.

Soon I heard noises from downstairs. It was

Jeff's voice. He sounded lively; he was talking vivaciously on the phone. Then a few minutes later I heard his steps on the stairs bounding up towards me.

And still I felt nothing.

'Sally! Sally! Open up.' The door handle rattled and turned, but the door didn't budge. I must have pulled the barrel bolt across, although I couldn't remember doing so. I stayed where I was, on the bathroom floor. 'Sally, open up! You'll wake Charlie if you don't.'

I got up and unfastened the bolt on the door.

'What's happened to your face? Oh Sally, poor you!' He held me by the shoulders and carefully scrutinised my face. I put my hand up to my lower left cheek. It was starting to swell, but still I felt nothing.

'You poor darling, you silly billy, my poor Sally. Did you walk into the doorpost?'

It was as if he'd forgotten he'd hit me; it was as if it were entirely my fault. It was as if the swelling of my face had nothing to do with his actions.

'I've got the job, Sally! Isn't that wonderful? I've got the job.'

I looked at his handsome face and could think of nothing to say.

'Oh cheer up, Sal, don't spoil it for me!' He kissed me. 'And guess what, they said how talented I am, and what a lovely family I've got.'

Still I said nothing.

'Let's go downstairs, Sal. We mustn't wake Charlie.'

Jeff took my hand and guided me downstairs

to the living room, and he sat me down on the sofa. Then he knelt on the floor in front of me.

'I'll get some champagne, Sal. That'll cheer you up.'

He lent forward and undid the buttons of my green and white striped shirt. As he lifted my breasts out of the nest of my bra, at last I began to feel something. I felt that my love was dead.

I looked down at his smooth blond head as he suckled at my breasts like a baby. He was a stranger to me, this man my husband. I did not know this man. Perhaps a dozen times he had struck me in six years of marriage, two blows for each year. Looking back on these incidents of violence, on each occasion it had been a small, apparently trivial, incident that had set him off. And each time it was the same story afterwards: he would make passionate love to me. To begin with I had thought this was because he was trying to wind back the clock, trying to restore us to the gentle love we had known at first.

At this instant I realised that this was the wrong explanation. Jeff's violence was the instinctive response of a weak man, a man who couldn't control his anger.

And was it really always the same story after an act of violence? While Jeff teased my nipples with his busy tongue, I realised that something new had emerged. Jeff now seemed to think that his violence was my fault, almost as if I had mutilated myself through some careless action like walking into a doorpost. It was almost as if he were merely the vehicle through which my clumsiness would be punished.

Jeff undressed me and I felt too passive to resist, although he was a stranger. And then I let this stranger fuck me, right there on the living room sofa.

22

NOW

Early Monday evening in Kentish Town and I'm sitting on my bed with a pile of unmarked assignments in front of me. There's no sign of my mother yet, though she promised she'd be back by five. Having her stay makes life easier. There is laughter every evening, the kitchen is always tidy and we never run out of anything. But I know without her telling me that she's ready to go home, to my father and their garden, to the familiarity of her own bed rather than the strangeness of the sofa bed in my study.

Though I love having my mother to stay, I did grumble to Charlie about having to move my work things out of my study before she arrived.

'That's a small price to pay,' Charlie told me, around a large mouthful of muesli. 'You're lucky having a study of your own most of the time. If you'd lent it to me for this year, you wouldn't have had to move out of it.'

'I bring in the bacon and I'm entitled to a study of my own,' I said rather too loudly, crashing crockery into the dishwasher in a staccato accompaniment.

Charlie looked puzzled at my grumpiness. 'I'm at the gateway of my career,' she said, trying to make me laugh with the imitation of her form mistress that usually has me in stitches. 'What I do in the next five or so years will have a more profound effect on my future than at any other time.'

I didn't even smile. 'You're too smart by half. I hope you're not trying to blackmail me into being even nicer to you than I already am.' I knew I was being unpleasant but couldn't keep the irritation out of my voice. Although after my last session with Helen I felt unburdened, this feeling lasted barely twenty-four hours. Since that time my life has felt out of control; too much is happening and yet nothing is happening.

'You'd think having this Blake bloke call you all the time would make you, like, happier,' Charlie said softly, as if she were talking to herself rather than me, but wanting me to hear nonetheless.

'That's got nothing to do with anything,' I said. 'Haven't you finished your cereal yet? It's gone eight o'clock.'

Poor Charlie didn't respond. She concentrated on finishing her breakfast and getting out of the house as quickly as possible.

★   ★   ★

I finish marking the set of assignments and put them away in my briefcase. When I open the bedroom door, Charlie is standing there on the landing, her hair concealed by the red bobble hat that she wears while she's studying. 'I got the parcel from Marge today,' she says. 'I would have told you earlier but you were too busy.'

126

Too busy? My heart starts to race so fast I can hear blood drumming in my ears. This is the moment I've been dreading for so long. Behind Charlie, on her bed, is a large padded envelope. Plastered with brightly coloured stamps and airmail stickers, it has already been ripped open. Suddenly dizzy, I seize hold of the banister. The palms of my hands are sweating.

'Are you OK, Mum? You've gone white.'

'I'm fine. What was in the envelope?'

'Lots of pictures.'

Photographs are piled on top of her desk. When I try to speak, my voice cracks. At the second attempt, I manage to say, 'Can I look at them?'

She nods and pulls out the chair for me to sit on. After wiping my damp hands on my skirt, I lift the photos and look underneath.

No newspaper clippings there.

'What are you looking for, Mum? Don't you want to see the photos?'

'Of course I do.' The twitch under my eye has started again. I begin to flick through the pictures with shaking fingers. There are dozens of them. Many are of Jeff when he was young. There is one of Jeff holding Charlie. He looks so young, younger than twenty-five. On his face is an expression of tenderness. Charlie is only a couple of weeks old, her features delicate, her head covered with the palest fuzz. I can feel that soft down on my lips now: I loved to caress her head with my mouth, to inhale the lovely freshly-bathed scent of her skin. I look more closely. There's a blob of sick on Jeff's arm next to

Charlie's mouth, and a dribble on his shoulder. How could I have forgotten that she was a colicky baby who cried a lot in those first few weeks?

I riffle through more photos. There are many of Jeff's parents, his stepmother Marge, and some cousins too. And there are a few of Jeff and Zoë, though not with the family. I didn't expect to see this. His arm is around her and they're smiling at the camera. There are palm trees behind them.

'I didn't know Zoë knew Dad.' Charlie is standing beside me.

'She was his friend first. I only met her later.' I stare at the photo, not wanting to meet Charlie's eye.

'After you met Dad?'

'Yes, after I met your father.'

'Funny that she's never said anything.'

'Why should she?'

'No reason.' Charlie hesitates before saying, 'There aren't any pictures of you, Mum. That's a bit funny. Didn't he like you?'

'Who?'

'Grandpa.'

'I don't think he did.'

After Jeff's funeral, his father and I lost touch, although he — and later Marge — sent Charlie a card and a fifty-dollar note every Christmas and birthday. At the funeral, looking bent and older than his years, he'd seemed distant, devastated. I recognised that my role was ambiguous to him. The separated wife who'd inherited Jeff's share of the house, and who was the mother of his grandchild. The separated wife who so tastelessly turned up for the funeral in the company of Zoë, whose photos he'd kept while keeping none of me.

'Was there anything else in the envelope, Charlie?'

'Only these pictures.'

'Any letters or stuff like that?'

'There was a nice note from Marge but that's all.'

No letters from Jeff. No newspaper cuttings. Relief washes over me. This is the time to tell her some more about the past. 'There's something I need to talk to you about,' I say. 'It's about . . . '

At this moment I hear the front door open and the click-clack of my mother's high-heels. 'Charlie!' She shouts up the stairs. 'Are you there, Charlie?'

'Hi Granny!' Charlie started calling her that as a joke a couple of years ago, instead of the *grandma* that my mother preferred, and it has stuck. 'Have you had a good day?'

'I've bought loads of lovely things. Would you like some coffee?'

'I'll be down in a minute.' Charlie puts an arm around my shoulders. 'What were you going to say?'

'Thanks for showing me your things, Charlie.' I feel a sense of reprieve; the parcel from Marge wasn't the disaster I'd feared. Tomorrow I'll tell Charlie about how her father died. Tomorrow night after my mother has gone.

Am I imagining an expression of disappointment on Charlie's face? Or is it relief? Perhaps I should wait for the weekend; I don't want a scene during the week. I kiss her cheek before running down the stairs.

23

NOW

The kitchen is cold and I turn up the central heating. My mother, still wearing her raincoat and a plaid scarf wound around her neck, is busying herself with the cafetière. She is surprised to see me home. I give her a big hug. She feels tiny even wrapped in her raincoat; I hope she isn't shrinking. 'I'll make the coffee,' I say. 'You sit down.'

'I'm not past it yet. You've been working all day. You sit down.'

Charlie comes bursting into the room, her hair still concealed by the bobble hat. She kisses her grandmother.

'Not Christmas yet, Charlie,' says my mother, clutching the bobble on her hat and yanking it off. Charlie laughs as her blonde hair falls around her face; suddenly she looks grown-up, much older than seventeen. She will be gone soon and my mother will be gone soon. But here we are, in this instant, three generations of women captured in almost tangible form in my mind, like insects in amber.

Charlie's cat Tico comes yowling into the kitchen. He wraps himself around my legs and deposits a few white hairs on my black tights.

'OK, Tico, time for your food.' I scrape some of his special minced meat into a bowl.

'Do you remember how you locked Tico up all those years ago, Charlie?' my mother says.

'Yes.' Charlie smiles: she and my mother love to reminisce. Charlie used to stay with my parents every half-term but gave that up just before her GCSE exams. In a way I'm sorry that she got too old for that. She used to love going down there and I loved the chance to be alone for a week too. They spoiled her rotten and allowed her to do almost anything she wanted, apart from take the boat out on her own.

My mother embarks on the story of how, years ago, Charlie and I couldn't find Tico. We searched everywhere until at last I heard a little mewing sound coming from Charlie's bedroom. There I found the kitten shut up in the drawer.

'Poor little Tico.' Charlie picks up the cat, who has finished his dinner. 'You know Gran, I didn't actually forget him.' When she stops stroking him, he immediately starts swishing his tail and looking offended. She peers out the kitchen window at our overgrown back garden. I watch her; she is going to tell her grandmother the truth about that day. 'I'd done something naughty,' Charlie says. 'I can't even remember what it was now.'

'Neither can I,' I add.

'And Mum decided to punish me by making me stay in my room for a while. So I took it out on poor Tico. And when Mum let me out, I thought I'd give her a bit of a shock by pretending Tico was lost, when I'd actually shut him in my drawer. I'm only surprised Mum hadn't heard him meowing before she did.'

'Direct transferral,' I tell my mother. 'I'd shut up Charlie so she locked up her little kitten. A funny thing, the human mind.' Charlie must have thought she was punishing me indirectly for punishing her.

I'd been horrified by that incident, a horror that was out of all proportion to the event. It had made me think of Jeff, although Jeff wouldn't have punished me obliquely. When I'd discovered Tico, I told Charlie what she'd done was nasty. She replied, with the logic she'd possessed from an early age, that what she'd done to Tico was no worse than what I'd done to her, shutting her up for an offence that neither of us can remember.

'Mum said what I'd done was cruel,' Charlie says. 'She told me I should guard against all violence.'

My mother and I exchange glances.

'Mum said I shouldn't ever hurt anyone who can't defend themselves. And yet I hadn't actually hurt Tico. And I never would.'

'I was worried that you might have, Charlie.' I lift the cat onto my lap and rub him under his chin. He starts to purr very loudly, his mouth slightly ajar in an undignified fashion. His breath smells of cat food.

My mother and Charlie embark on another long anecdote. I let their conversation wash over me, and only half-listen to its ebb and flow. For some reason I start thinking of the last time I saw Celia. She'd guessed by that time what my marriage was like.

But I never did have a chance to talk to her about it.

24

THEN

Celia lived in the old section of the residential care home. It had once been a private house, a nineteenth-century Gothic revival structure of some thirty rooms. Its exterior was a mass of gables and roof planes, pierced by a forest of tall chimneys, each of a unique design. Yet the whole was given a surprising unity by the round tower, placed at the peak of the roofs, and capped by a bulbous dome sheeted in scalloped slates. The building's fragmented nature must have made its conversion difficult. Inside, convoluted passage-ways disorientated the visitor and frustrated the staff. Yet the old part of the home lacked the institutional character of the new wing. This had been added at the back by an architect sensitive enough only to perceive the hideous nature of their design and to conceal it from public view.

Celia's room was painted in shades of pink. I found it oppressive: the pink absorbed the light and made everything appear dingy. Celia lay propped up on three pillows. All the flesh had gone from her face: it looked very close to being a skull, and her thin yellow skin was stretched across the fine bone structure. Her hair had recently been set. Tight blue curls framed her face and clashed with the different blue of her eyes. Jeff kissed her wrinkled hand that was gnarled with arthritis; it must have been a couple of years since he'd last seen her. At first Charlie stood back from the bed but Celia beckoned her forward and Charlie moved closer.

'Hello, my dear,' Celia said.

'Hello.' Charlie's voice was solemn. I thought how old Celia's ninety-one years must seem to a five-year-old.

Celia looked at Jeff. She had always been fond of men. But now she was no longer able to sparkle for anyone, even my handsome husband.

'How are you?' Jeff said.

Celia grimaced.

'Jeff's practice is doing really well.' I felt it necessary to intervene, whether to protect my husband or Celia was unclear.

Celia's taut skin loosened sufficiently to allow her to pucker her forehead with intense concentration. It was an effort but she managed to say, 'How nice for him.' Abruptly the words jerked out. Charlie giggled. Celia looked at her in amazement.

'Give Charlotte some sweets,' she said, much as one might suggest that monkeys at the zoo be given peanuts. 'Then send her outside into the garden.'

'I'll take her out in a minute,' Jeff said quickly.

'But what about the sweets?' Charlie looked hopefully at Celia.

'I haven't got any.' I said. 'Give Celia a kiss.'

'I'm not senile,' Celia said. 'There are some in my locker.'

I gave Charlie two black and white striped humbugs.

'I've never believed in over-indulgence for the young,' Celia said. 'It's only when you reach the peak and start the downhill run that you should over-indulge. And that's merely to distract you from what you suspect lies at the bottom. When you reach the bottom, there's no point in any sort of indulgence.' She was muttering quickly to herself. Her words were hard to catch and she seemed to have forgotten our presence. I exchanged glances with Jeff.

'I'll take Charlie out into the garden,' he said.

'It's been nice to see you, Jeffrey.' Celia held out her hand. Jeff took it in his before kissing her cheek. 'I do hope you enjoy your new job,' she said before shutting her eyes.

'Would you like me to stay on for a while?' I asked.

'Yes.' Celia opened her eyes again and looked at me with her piercing blue eyes. 'What are you thinking of?'

I felt disconcerted, as I'd been thinking about death. I switched my train of thought onto a different track and began to tell her some little anecdotes about my life.

In the middle of one of these she interrupted me, as if she hadn't heard a word, or perhaps she was simply bored. 'Why don't you go back to university?'

Too surprised to do more than let my mouth hang open, I stared at her.

'Your mother told me you're having trouble finding a job. But you've got a first-class degree. You're much too smart to be wasting your time now Charlotte is at school. Why don't you do some postgraduate work?' She had certainly not lost her old perspicacity.

'You know, I've been thinking the same thing.' I paused, and rested my hand on hers. 'It's the sort of work I could easily do while Charlie's at school. And today I got the offer of a postgraduate studentship.'

'Did you? Well done! Take it. Don't always do what other people expect of you. *Especially Jeff.*'

The inflexion in her voice when she spoke the last two words was impossible to miss and it came as a great surprise. For years I'd assumed that she liked my handsome blond husband but now I began to have my doubts.

'You always were the loyal child,' she said, 'and very inclined to protect people. Think of your cousin when I took the two of you to the zoo. He pushed you over, it was as clear as anything, but you said it was your fault. You need to protect yourself too, Sally.'

I held her hand and wondered if I should tell her what Jeff was really like. I was preparing the words when she began to mumble. It was impossible to make any sense of what she was saying. She seemed to have lapsed into confused memories that meant nothing to me. I made noises of agreement as she murmured on, but it soon became clear that she was no longer aware of my presence. Gradually her muttering petered out. She was almost asleep. I looked at my watch. It was time to leave.

'I must go,' I said distinctly. 'Jeff has a meeting with some prospective clients on the way back.'

Celia started, and looked up at me in

astonishment. 'I thought you'd gone already.' She pulled the bedclothes up to her chin with her claw-like hands, as if she'd been surprised in a condition of exposure.

'Goodbye, my dear,' she said in a sprightly manner.

I kissed her forehead. Her skin felt like paper and was very cold. I turned back when I reached the doorway. She was watching me. I waved and blew her a kiss. She waved back, like a small child full of wonder. Her expression moved me almost to tears and I had a feeling this would be the last time I would ever see her.

Yet I wouldn't have wished upon her a long period of confinement in a bed in a care home. I thought of my mother, who would be turning sixty soon, and my father who was about to retire. Once Celia went, my parent's generation would be next in line for the grave. That thought filled me with a sense of loss, followed almost at once by panic; it was as if I had stepped onto an express train and was speeding towards infinity. In the corridor I wiped my eyes and filled my lungs with air that smelled of roast mutton and Brussels sprouts, mingled with disinfectant.

I found Jeff and Charlie in the gardens at the front of the house. Jeff was parading up and down the lawn, while Charlie ran about showing off for the benefit of a group of old women sitting in a conservatory at the side of the house. The women nodded benevolently at her. As I approached, Jeff barked an order at Charlie. She appeared instantly, causing more nods of approval from the spectators at the sight of her obedience.

'I'm running late,' he said sharply.

'It's half-past four. We've got plenty of time to get to the Fosters.'

Jeff didn't deign to reply. When we reached the car, I opened the door for Charlie and buckled her into her seat. Jeff started the engine and Charlie fell asleep almost at once.

'I hope I don't end up like Celia,' Jeff said, accelerating.

'How do you want to end up?' The panic I'd felt a few moments before returned and my heart began to skitter. I wanted to jump out of this vehicle that was hurtling me towards the future. I wanted to grab Charlie and leap out, to make a run for it while I could. But I knew I never would. I didn't have the guts for it.

'Sailing around the world on a yacht,' Jeff said. 'Having a heart attack asleep in my bunk one night.'

'That's very romantic.' I was surprised that my voice was steady when my pulses were racing and my palms clammy. He appeared to have forgotten our boat trip to La Spezia for our honeymoon. That incident of violence was the first of so many random acts of anger, of petulance.

'And what about you? I'm sure you've got your ending all mapped out.' His tone was mocking.

'I don't know how I'd like to end up.'

'How unlike you not to have an answer. You've got one for every occasion.'

'Do I? How unbearable. Perhaps I'm going into a decline.'

Jeff laughed. 'You could follow Celia's axiom

and indulge yourself. But maybe you do that already, by being too morbid.'

'You sound bitter.' Perhaps he was also affected by our visit to Celia. Maybe it reminded him of his own mortality. 'Do I make your life so unpleasant?'

'No. I love you actually.'

'Why?' I was surprised by what he had said. Neither of us had mentioned love for some time.

'Habit.'

'Do you think we should separate?' The words slipped out of my mouth, without conscious formulation in my brain. Although I'd thought of this as a possibility many times before, I immediately regretted mentioning it. Long ago I had decided to stay with him, because of Charlie. I wanted her to have a family that lived together. A normal family, if there was such a thing. A family with two parents who would see her every day.

But Jeff seemed to be unfazed by my question. 'No.' He sounded sure of his answer, but his calm certainty made me think that he had thought about this before. 'There's too much at stake.'

'What?'

'Our house. Charlie. The relationship we've built up over the years. And I'd hate to have to start all over again.'

'Charlie. Yes, there's Charlie.'

'Are you happy, Sally?'

Jeff had never asked me this before, and I felt surprised. 'It's sad that Celia's dying like this; all on her own in a home full of ancient people. I'd always thought she'd had a good life until she started talking like that this afternoon.' I paused while Jeff negotiated us out of the slip road and onto the motorway. 'Mum is finding this all very difficult, you know. Celia's always been her favourite aunt, and she's the only one of that generation left.'

We drove on in silence for a while. 'You've not mentioned yourself. What about you?' Jeff said. 'Are you happy with your life?'

'I'm sad about Celia, but other things are OK.'

'What?'

'Charlie and all that.'

I found it impossible to say what he may have wanted to hear: that I was happy with him. I was unhappy with him, but also suspected that one could never hope to be completely content in a relationship. I certainly didn't want to tell him yet about the idea of postgraduate work. It seemed that I no longer had the ability to make up my own mind about anything but waited passively until I was told what to do. Was it fear of what his reaction might be? Or was it a lack of character on my part? I didn't have the answers to any of these questions. But I felt calmer at the thought of being a student again.

'That's really peculiar,' Jeff said, his tone sarcastic. 'Here you are with a marvellous opportunity to be unhappy. After all, Celia is dying, and we've squabbled all afternoon. And now you tell me that you're OK.'

'You sound aggrieved,' I said. 'As if I shouldn't be.'

Jeff didn't reply at once. He directed his

attention to some skilful changing of lanes to enable our car to move four places up the queue of traffic. Pleased with this achievement, he turned to me. 'We'll be there in five minutes. Do try and be your usual charming self when we meet these clients, Sally. This could be a good job. The Fosters have got good taste as well as a lot of money. And for Christ's sake, keep Charlie under control.'

Keep Charlie under control. Yes, that was important. But what the hell was Jeff doing about keeping himself under control?

25

NOW

A wind has sprung up and is rattling the kitchen window frames. Charlie and my mother are still embroidering anecdotes while I have been transported to Buckinghamshire and back. Now they are reminiscing about the day that Charlie and the son of the Coverack inn-keeper almost succeeded in launching my father's boat.

The dining room clock strikes half six. 'Time to think about what we're going to eat.' I jump to my feet.

'What about a glass of something first?' Charlie says, winking at me. Her grandmother is very fond of a little tipple as she calls it. I get out the bottle of white wine I put in the refrigerator this morning.

'Lovely idea, Charlie,' says my mother with alacrity. 'Will you join me?'

'No. I've got to do a bit more homework after dinner. I'm sure Mum will though. And I'll sit with you while you knock back a glass.'

'You're so crude, Charlie. I sip wine, I don't knock it back.'

'Very lady-like, Gran. Would you like to see some photos Marge sent me?'

'Marge, your step-grandmother?'

'The very one. They came today.'

I open the bottle and pour two glasses. 'Drink

it upstairs,' I tell my mother. She looks tired and will be more comfortable in an armchair talking to her beloved Charlie. But I'm not being entirely altruistic; I don't want to hear them talking about the photos and I'm expecting Anthony to call shortly. If my mother overhears the conversation she'll be full of questions.

'The Blake bloke'll be ringing soon,' says Charlie, as if she can read my mind. 'So she wants to be alone.'

'Who's the Blake bloke, Sally?'

'Awesome new admirer,' says Charlie, grinning. 'He's in the States at the moment. Phones every second night. Like, at seven o'clock on the dot. You were out the other night, Granny, when he rang.'

'Does he live there?'

'No,' I say. 'He's just a friend. He's working there this term.' I busy myself extracting vegetables from the bottom shelf of the refrigerator. The conversation behind me has a life of its own, with or without my involvement.

'How old is he?' my mother says, switching her interrogation to Charlie.

'Dunno Gran.'

'Charlie!'

'I don't know. I haven't seen him. Mum knows. Ancient, I expect.'

'Ancient like your mother?'

'Probably.'

'What does that make me?'

'Antediluvian!'

While I can't help laughing, I've had enough of them both. 'Off you go now,' I say, clapping

144

my hands like I used to when Charlie was a child and I was shooing her out of the way. 'You can entertain each other in the living room while I get on with cooking.'

Alone in the kitchen I start to make dinner. Preparing vegetables is a form of therapy; cutting up the onions and braising them slowly in olive oil; slicing through the fleshy courgettes; arranging the cod pieces on the bed of vegetables and pouring over the top a sauce of coarsely chopped tomatoes and herbs. I am placing the dish in the oven when the phone starts ringing. Involuntarily I look at my watch. Seven o'clock precisely. Impeccable timing.

As I wash my hands, I hear my mother's footsteps overhead, clicking to the phone in the living room. I run to the downstairs phone and pick up the receiver; I'm too late, my mother is speaking on the upstairs extension.

'Yes, Sally is at home. I'll get her for you. Whom shall I say is calling?' My mother pauses and I hear Anthony's voice saying his first name. I should speak now but I'm curious to hear if my mother will be able to think of a reason for continuing the conversation. I'm not disappointed. 'Anthony who?' she says, although she already knows his second name. It's time for me to break in. I say 'Hello.'

'Sally, you've reached the extension.' My mother's voice is as gay as if she's hosting a drinks party. 'That's lovely, just in time. I'm Sally's mother, Anthony. Goodbye.' There is a little click as she hangs up.

'So you've met my mother.' I shut my eyes so I

can concentrate on Anthony's voice. I find that I am laughing; because of my mother and because it's Anthony on the line again.

'I've missed you,' he says. 'It seems like more than forty-eight hours since we spoke last.'

I sit down on the floor and lean against the wall. Peace at last; the sound of Anthony's voice and the smell of dinner cooking.

26

THEN

Jeff picked me up from our house in Islington a few minutes before three o'clock; I could tell he was pleased that I'd put on the navy blue dress he'd bought me for my birthday and a smart pair of heels that I rarely wore. Charlie's school was not far away but to save time we drove to collect her. All three of us, Jeff, Charlie and me, were to visit Celia in the care home in Buckinghamshire. Afterwards we were to meet the Fosters.

Normally I would visit Celia once a month on my own at the weekend, leaving Charlie with Jeff. Celia was not easy with very small children, perhaps because she'd had none of her own. But Jeff always was keen on any opportunity to kill two birds with the one stone, as he put it. His potential clients, Mr and Mrs Foster, lived not far from Celia. Jeff had started his design business nearly three years ago. We had a huge mortgage and were finding it a struggle to make ends meet, and getting this new job was important to him. He also thought that bringing Charlie and me to meet the clients might swing things in his favour.

Jeff and I were early at the school, but so too were many other parents, mothers mainly. Cars lined both sides of the road, many of them on the yellow zigzag road-markings prohibiting parking. It was a bleak March day and the low grey sky drained the colour out of everything. At the gates to the school, a small crowd of women waited. I suppose it was the weather that made them look depressed, like wives and girlfriends clustering around a pithead after a mining disaster. Although I joined them, I didn't feel like chatting that day. With Jeff waiting impatiently in the car it was important to be ready to make a quick getaway.

When the doors to the school opened, the first wave of small children surged out. Charlie was one of them and I watched her race across the schoolyard: the crotch of her tights had descended during the day to the level of her knees but that didn't seem to handicap her. I held out my arms for her to jump into. We hugged and I took her bag, and kissed her smooth round cheek. She looked tired, with dark crescents under her eyes; this was her first year at school. Her pale blonde hair, smooth like her father's, was always neat, even after she'd just woken, but she lacked his natural tidiness. Her grey school tights had a hole in one knee, which hadn't been there that morning, and a fresh piece of Elastoplast covered the perennial wound on her kneecap. The accident that had torn her tights must also have ripped the cotton thread holding up her hem, for a deep pocket drooped down to one side of her tunic. She was wearing her school jumper inside out: the label stuck out behind her like Paddington Bear's: *PLEASE LOOK AFTER THIS CHILD THANK YOU*. Her face answered my inspection with an innocent beam; she was oblivious of her dishevelled appearance. It was impossible not to smile back.

Hand-in-hand we hurried to the car. Jeff had parked it in front of the others in the street and the engine was running. I strapped Charlie into the back and climbed into my own seat. Jeff was already pulling away while I was shutting the door.

'Have you got any other clothes for her?' Jeff said. 'Those tights look a bit of a mess. What happened, Charlie? Did you fall over again?'

Charlie began to describe in great detail what had happened to her. Something to do with her second-best friend and a boy from the year above who'd picked on her third-best friend, and how in the ensuing scuffle she'd fallen over and torn her tights.

'I've got some clean clothes,' I told Jeff when she'd finished. I knew that our appearance would matter when we visited the prospective clients; an up-and-coming designer shouldn't have a family dressed in rags. 'But Celia won't mind. She's past caring for appearances now, if she ever did.'

'Why is Celia past caring for appearances?' asked Charlie.

'Because she's old and tired. And she's always thought that how you behave is more important than how you look,' I said.

'Because she's going to die very soon,' said Jeff at the same. He glanced at me, and I narrowed my eyes in warning. I'd wanted Charlie to learn about Celia's imminent death gradually.

'Why is she going to die very soon?' Charlie said.

There was a short silence. I waited for Jeff to reply. When it became obvious that he wasn't going to, I said: 'Because she's very old.'

'Does she want to die?' Charlie's voice was anxious.

'I think so.'

'Why?'

'Because she's old. Because she's had a very good life, but now she's come to the end of it, just as we all must. And because she's too weak to cope with living any longer.'

There was a pause. Perhaps Jeff's right, I thought. This is the time to discuss death with Charlie.

'Will she go somewhere after she dies?' Charlie said after a couple of minutes.

'We don't know. Some people say there's a heaven, and that the spirit of the person goes there after the body dies. But some people think there's nothing after death, that people simply die, and the spirit dies with them. But no-one knows for sure.'

'What's nothing when you die?'

This was a difficult one. 'Nothing is when the spirit isn't living any more. The spirit's the bit inside you that thinks and feels.'

'But if Celia dies and is nothing, we remember her,' Charlie said. 'And we're still living. So she can't be nothing.'

The conversation was becoming complex. I hesitated before replying. 'Yes, you're right, Charlie. As long as those of us who've known Celia are alive, she'll be living in our memories. But to Celia after death, she'd be nothing, because her spirit and body would be no more. That's if there's no heaven. No one knows if there's a heaven or not.'

'What do you think, Mummy?'

'I don't know, cherub. I'm agnostic.'

'Agnostic.' Charlie repeated the word carefully. Her vocabulary was expanding rapidly and it was clear that she liked the sound of this new word. 'What's agnostic?'

'Not knowing about something for sure. And recognising that you don't know.'

After a minute's silence Charlie said: 'I don't want to die.'

'You won't for a long, long time.'

'You shouldn't think about it anyway,' said Jeff.

I felt annoyed with him. 'How can you tell her that, when you brought up the subject yourself?' I whispered.

'I believe in telling the truth,' Jeff said sharply. 'Besides, there's no need to complicate things by suggesting there's nothing after death.'

'You're being inconsistent. If you tell the truth about facts, you've also got to try to tell the truth about abstractions.'

'How can we, when we don't know of any definite truth about them? It's better not to confuse Charlie by mixing up what's real with what's unknown.'

'But children are interested in these things. I was obsessed with the idea of infinity when I was a kid.'

'That's typical.'

In the back seat Charlie seemed to have

become bored with our discussion. Gazing out of the window, she looked as if she were miles away, but she could well have been mulling over what we'd been talking about. I took a CD out of the glove box and slipped it into the player. I wanted to distract Charlie from what was threatening to develop into an argument between Jeff and me. We'd had quite a few of those from very early on in our marriage. After seven years I understood enough of Jeff's character to know that whenever he was worried about something it was best to keep a low profile. But today I found it impossible to let the conversation die.

'Any child with an inquiring mind is bound to ask at some stage what comes after death,' I said.

'You could've just said heaven.'

'But that's untrue! We don't know if there's a heaven. How can I say it's heaven, if there mightn't be one?'

'She'll find out when she's old enough to cope.'

The intensity of our irritation with each other was out of all proportion to the issue, but like a dog with a bone I couldn't let the conversation alone. 'Isn't it better to encourage her to think for herself instead of depending on convention?'

Jeff moved into the fast lane. The speedometer showed that we were travelling at eighty-five miles an hour. I looked out the side window at the cars we were passing: most were going above the speed limit.

'As far as I'm concerned, the matter's closed.' Jeff's voice was tight with anger. 'I don't want to hear any more about it.'

'There you are. Down go the shutters. inconvenient topic comes up and you want to slam a cover over the lot.'

Jeff kept his eyes on the road ahead. The rigidity of his body indicated his displeasure. In the back seat Charlie happily carolled an accompaniment to the music from the CD.

Jeff and I sat on, in a silence reverberating with our discontent.

27

NOW

Every time I see Kate, she asks me where my photograph is. 'I want to finish the departmental website,' she says, laughing with less and less mirth as the days go by and I still haven't delivered. 'It's one of my Key Performance Indicators. I want it by tomorrow at the very latest.'

After dinner, when Charlie has gone upstairs to work on an essay and my mother is having a rest, I take my laptop into the living room and trawl through the photos in the 'My Pictures' directory. I'd swear there are some portrait photos of me somewhere on the laptop but they certainly aren't where they should be. All the pics I can find are either landscapes or pictures of Charlie. So much for my hope of avoiding the college photographer, the technician with a gift for turning animated human faces into expressionless masks.

My mother comes downstairs as I am pulling our most recent photograph album out of the bookshelves. It is the one I made a year or two ago, even though hard copies no longer seem relevant, not when digital copies of our photos should be on my laptop. Of course my mother wants to join in the search. We sit together on the sofa and trawl through the pages.

'That might do.' My mother points to a picture of me taken two years before. My hair was shorter then, but this doesn't matter. Anyone looking at this image would be able to recognise me. It's the hair colour and the eyes, and that goofy grin that shows most of my upper teeth.

'I took this.' My mother is pleased with herself. 'It's a good likeness and I love that white silk shirt with the navy blue blazer. It makes you look very professional.'

I detach the picture from the page and put it to one side.

'This is fun,' my mother says. 'Let's look at some more.'

I lift out some of the older albums. We start with the one my parents gave me recently, dating from when I was young, from when they were young. As my mother and I work through them, I wonder if my earliest memories may in fact not be memories at all, but simply suggestions absorbed into my receptive mind from photos my parents took of my earliest childhood. I remember this eighteen-month-old Sally standing with a bucket and spade on a beach in Cornwall. I was there, I felt the sand between my toes, I felt the cool breeze on my skin, I smiled at the person taking the picture.

The power of imagination; I couldn't possibly have remembered events this early, or this clearly. I've seen the photo again and again over the years and that's what is in my memory. What is real, what is imagined? I don't want to think about this.

'You're in a daydream, Sally.' My mother

nudges me gently and flips over to the next page. 'Look, here's a photo that got away. It's that flat you had after you and Jeff separated.'

I picked it up. It must have fallen out of one of the more recent albums. The flat was cheap and dingy, and was on the upper floor of a terraced house in Kentish Town. It was the flat that Charlie and I had moved into after we left Jeff.

'I expect it's long since been gentrified, Sally,' my mother said, slipping the picture back into the album and turning over another page. 'Hard to believe that was ten years ago. It had a very nice entrance hall, as I recall.'

That staircase. I will never forget it. It rose steeply from the entrance hall laid with its beautiful encaustic tiles that were so popular in Victorian houses. I shudder to think of that floor now, with its geometric design of red and brown and white tiles, interspersed with the occasional blue. How hard those tiles were, and how much damage they could do. The staircase was too steep and narrow for such a fancy hall; the treads small, the risers high.

★ ★ ★

After I'd left Jeff, it had been a dispiriting exercise searching for somewhere to rent. I didn't have much money; all I had was my studentship and a small amount in my bank account. In the meantime I borrowed from my parents.

The strange thing was that Jeff wanted Charlie

and me to come back. He thought we could continue as if nothing had changed. But after seeing him *in flagrante delicto*, I'd made up my mind our marriage was over. Nothing would change that, not all the appeals in the world.

I'd spent a few days flat-hunting before I managed to find a place that was not too far from where we'd been living, so that Charlie wouldn't need to change schools. I wanted her to have some continuity in her life. It wasn't until later that I changed our last name from Hector to Lachlan; not until after Jeff had beaten up Zoë and I decided that Charlie and I had to escape London for a while.

It had been a nightmare moving my stuff into the new flat. It wasn't only the physical exertion of hauling boxes in and out; it was also the grief that occasionally struck me, that this was how our once-happy marriage had ended. My agonising over what to take and what to leave behind didn't help either. Every object had a memory, nothing was without a past, and all of it hurt. In the end I decided it would be better not to care and that made the task easier. I took what friends had given me together with a few basic things that Charlie and I would need in our new home.

On my second journey up that steep staircase the bottom came out of the cardboard box I was carrying. The contents fell out, evading my snatching hands. The crystal wineglasses I'd inherited from Celia and the lovely glass vase Alessandra had given me for my birthday bounced down the stairs and smashed into a hundred pieces on the tiled floor below. One of the tiles had a small chip out of it. I hoped the landlord wouldn't notice. He seemed the sort who might.

★ ★ ★

My mother is holding up the photo album and pointing to a picture. She is laughing at herself; she is laughing at the sight of herself as a three-year-old girl sitting on her Aunt Celia's lap. Although my mother says that Celia never took much notice of her until she was ten or so, the bond between them is evident here. She must have been wriggling when it was taken; Celia looks more as if she is restraining her rather than holding her.

Closely I examine my mother's face in the photo. She was such a pretty child with her fair curls and her angelic expression. Then I look at Celia. I had always been very fond of her. My maternal grandmother died when I was small and Celia had filled her place, although she was much older than my grandmother. In the picture her head is half-turned towards the camera, showing her strong profile.

Suddenly I realise who it was that Anthony reminded me of when I sat next to him on the plane. It was Celia. The likeness is in the nose, the strong Roman nose, and in the slightly heart-shaped jaw line. Celia's eyes are downcast in the photograph, which is anyway not in colour. But her eyes were a vivid piercing blue, just like Anthony's.

'Anthony looks a bit like Celia,' I tell my mother.

'It would be good to keep that nose in the family,' she says, laughing again and for rather too long. When she sees my face, she adds, 'You didn't hear me make that remark, Sally.'

28

NOW

Tuesday morning again and I struggle out of bed. I have to be awake enough to talk to Helen, alert enough to be coherent. The strain is beginning to tell; the strain of the early-morning rising, the strain of talking about myself incessantly, endlessly rehashing the past. The twitch under my right eye doesn't seem to be noticeable so far. Standing in front of the bathroom mirror, I watch as I feel the nervous spasm. Some nerve is jumping just below the surface; it's surprising that its effect on the muscle isn't visible.

I creep out of the house, hoping not to disturb my mother. 'I've got an eight o'clock doctor's appointment in Hampstead,' I told her last night. My mother doesn't need to know that her daughter is seeing a shrink. I tell her only of my successes, never my failures. She knows of my principal failure of course: my marriage to Jeff. She knows of his unfaithfulness and his violence. But I want to protect her from the knowledge that this has left such a lasting legacy.

'Nothing wrong, I hope?' my mother said.

'I just need to renew a prescription. I'll drive there and then take you to Paddington Station straight afterwards.'

'You're much too busy, Sally,' she said. 'I

could just as easily take a cab.'

But I couldn't bear to think of her making her way there alone, with her heavy suitcase and the extra parcels from her shopping in London; those little extravagances that she can't buy in Helston or Penzance.

It's yet another overcast autumn day, the sky the colour of old pewter with not even a faint gleam where the sun should be. The traffic is unexpectedly heavy. Although in my car at half-past seven, thirty-five minutes later I'm cruising up and down Helen's street looking for a parking space. At last I see a man shutting the front door of a house a few hundred metres from Helen's. Slowly, as if he has all the time in the world, as if I'm not waiting right behind him, he climbs into his car and drives off. I pull into the space. As I get out of the car, it starts raining, unusually heavy for London. Although I don't have an umbrella, I can't summon up the energy to run.

Because I'm late, I feel even more out of control, even more at the mercy of Helen. She will forgive me of course. It's all the same to her, late or early, it's all the same. I'm merely one of the many lost souls on whom she looks down benignly, beatifically.

In Helen's consulting room, I kick off my shoes and prostrate myself on the sofa. Fifty minutes lying flat on my back — forty minutes today because I'm so late — would be a luxury if I didn't have to perform. And I'm determined to finish telling Helen about Jeff; about everything that happened after he assaulted Zoë.

161

But it's hard to begin, so hard to begin. Where shall I start? I should be logical, I should be consistent; I should start where I left off last Tuesday morning. I shall tell Helen what happened to Charlie and me after Jeff's attack on Zoë hit the news-papers, after the beginning of my friendship with Zoë.

Instead I begin to talk about Anthony.

'It's hard to believe it's barely four weeks since I met him.' I hold my fingernails up in front of my face for inspection, a common practice when I begin a session with Helen. I wonder to myself, who is this person who has begun to blather to her shrink about her boyfriend. But I proceed relentlessly. 'It seems as if I've known him forever.'

'Yes.'

'I wish he could be here for Jim's birthday party this Saturday. He's my friend Kate's partner. She's hired a canal boat to take us out.'

Helen says nothing. I'm not surprised. She knows I'm procrastinating. But I think of how Anthony and I are getting to know each other with our long phone conversations, and how we like what we are discovering. Maybe we are lucky being able to get to know each other like this, on the phone, with no anxiety yet about the physical side of things, just chat. He tells me about his day and I tell him about mine. We talk a lot about our work, but we each reveal bits of our past too, gradually, gently, incrementally. Maybe this is what my sessions with Helen should be like.

But my phone conversation with Anthony last

night was different. I decide not to tell Helen of Anthony's news — that one of the US colleagues with whom he is collaborating has decided to accept a chair at Cambridge. This will reduce the probability that Anthony might move permanently to the US, I reckon, but there's no need for Helen to know this.

Perhaps I wouldn't consider letting Anthony into my life if it were not for my sessions with Helen. That would probably be her view. But of course I'm simply projecting opinions onto her. She gives little away. I examine my fingernails again for inspiration. I really must file that thumbnail into shape.

'After I met Zoë I felt much stronger,' I tell her. My subconscious has fooled my conscious self, has taken it by surprise. This new information erupts unexpectedly, as if it is magma that has found a weak point in the Earth's crust. 'I knew that Zoë was braver than me. She'd experienced something similar to me but she'd had the courage to take a strong line.' I'm drawing breath to continue the flow when Helen interrupts.

'You felt that you couldn't have deserved Jeff's violence if Zoë had experienced it too?' Helen is back with her old obsession.

'No, that wasn't it at all. You know perfectly well I don't think I deserved to be struck by Jeff. That might be your opinion but it's not mine.'

I realise that I am no longer angered by Helen's view, even though I think she is wrong. I never believed I deserved Jeff's violence. I tell her, 'It was more that after meeting Zoë I no longer felt so isolated. I felt there was someone I could talk to about Jeff. I wasn't on my own any longer.'

Helen jots something down on her writing pad. I hear her pen scratching over the paper.

'I chose to stay and later I chose to go,' I continue after a while. 'And the catalyst to my going certainly was that woman I'd seen making love to Jeff.' I almost say fucking but insert love-making at the last second. I try not to think too much about that incident, I try not to think of Jeff's expression as he saw me with the woman who turned out to be Zoë. 'But Jeff's assault of Zoë made a bond between us. We were connected because she'd shared my experience and we could talk about it.'

'Were you glad that Zoë had been punished by Jeff? She had stolen your husband, after all.'

Now that Helen has raised this question, it seems like an obvious one. The curious thing is that it has never occurred to me before. Was I glad? I have to think carefully. How different our lives might have been if Jeff hadn't attacked her.

'Were you glad?' Helen repeats.

'Maybe I was, at some unconscious level. Maybe Jeff's attack on Zoë made it easier for me to forgive her.' I hesitate, once more wondering why I'd never thought of this before. 'I didn't really have much time to think. All I felt was sympathy for Zoë and a desire to shield Charlie. And so much happened afterwards.'

Helen says nothing. I begin to tell her about my conversation with Jeff when he phoned me at my parents' place in Coverack, the day he was bailed out of jail. When I finish speaking, she clears her throat. I've almost forgotten her presence, so caught up am I in the past. 'So he was asking for your sympathy. And did you give him any, Sally?' Her voice is gentle.

'I wasn't in the least bit sympathetic. Not that it mattered. He wasn't listening. He was talking for his own benefit, to justify himself.'

'Yes.'

'And that was one of the last times I ever spoke to him, Helen. He died not long afterwards.'

'Did you regret your lack of sympathy after that?'

'I've never regretted it,' I say immediately. I don't tell Helen that I've occasionally asked myself this same question and always the answer has been the same: Jeff deserved no sympathy. 'I couldn't have encouraged him in his self-delusion. He was getting worse, not better.'

'I'm afraid we're going to have to stop there, Sally.'

I feel disorientated as I get to my feet, almost as if I have arisen from the sofa into another time period. Helen smiles at me as she holds the door open, a smile of astonishing sweetness. She is an enigma, my Helen; and our professional relationship guarantees that she stays this way.

Outside, I pass by a young woman as she is turning into Helen's tiny front garden. I turn and watch as she presses the buzzer on the intercom. Helen's voice bids her enter, the door clicks open and she is swallowed up. Helen's day is full of the damaged, the affluent damaged, seven or eight sessions. The miracle is that she remembers us all. Although perhaps she doesn't; after all, her response is rarely more than a yes or a no. Those in analysis are analysing themselves.

We are nearly there, Helen and I; we are nearly through. We have peeled the layers from the past as if pulling the petals off a tightly furled rosebud, stripping it petal by petal.

But we don't need to go right down to the very centre. Helen doesn't need to know everything that has happened to me. There are some things that I will never tell her.

29

NOW

When I shut Helen's front door, I shut up the past. I have to push hard. Against those things that happened the last time I saw Jeff alive, for instance. They're never going to be let out, not if I can help it.

Hurrying to South End Green, I slip on some wet leaves and fall to my knees. A smiling old lady helps me up; the irony isn't lost on either of us. But what am I doing at the bus stop? Time is shrinking too fast, clasping me in its tight embrace. I begin to run back to the car, parked in Helen's street. I have to get my mother to Paddington for the ten o'clock Inter-City. Even though I know a number of shortcuts, it will still be a rush and after dropping her off. I'll have to dash back in time to give a two-hour lecture.

It's twenty past nine when I turn into Trafalgar Terrace. There's no time for coffee. It's as well my mother has her return ticket; we won't lose precious time queuing at Paddington. And there she is, standing on the front porch, surrounded by parcels and holding her suitcase. She looks small, vulnerable even; but this is misleading. She has always known what she's doing. When she sees me, she waves. I double-park outside the house, and help her and her belongings into the car.

'Sweet of you to drive me,' she says, fastening her seatbelt. 'I know you're very busy.'

'It's fine, Mum.' I try to keep any trace of impatience out of my voice. This must be the fifth time we've had this conversation.

'But it gives me a chance to ask you something,' my mother says.

'What's been wrong with the past five days? No chance then?' I smile at her; I can guess what is coming next.

'This Anthony,' she says. 'He sounded pleasant on the phone.'

'How could you tell? You only spoke to him for a minute.'

'Lovely voice.'

'Lovely accent. You're a bit of a snob, Mum.'

She laughs as I hoped she might. I want to deflect her from the impending interrogation.

'Lovely manners, Sally. You interrupted us.'

'He was calling long distance, to speak to me.'

'Yes, phoning every two days from the States, Charlie said.'

'He's on leave there for a term. Well, actually he's working with someone there, so that's why he chose to go to Harvard.' I negotiate the turn onto a side street where there isn't so much traffic before adding, 'He's visiting the cellular and molecular biology department there.'

'Same field as you then. How old is he?'

'Forty.'

'What does he work on?'

'Genetics. But he's specialised in cloning. I'm glad I got to the phone last night in time to stop you grilling him!'

My mother doesn't reply. I steal a glance at her; she is looking out the side window and her thick white hair obscures her face.

'Cloning, eh,' she says eventually. 'Such a funny thing. I sometimes wonder what it would be like to have a clone of oneself instead of a biological child.'

'It wouldn't be exactly the same as you,' I tell her. 'People don't realise that differences in the environment of the womb, what the mother eats and so on, can have a big impact on the embryo. So even at birth it wouldn't be the same.'

'Upbringing too, I suppose.'

'Yes.' I glance at my mother, who is smiling benevolently at me.

'Think how strong the temptation would be with one's clone to load it up with advice,' my mother says.

'Why would you do that?'

'Because with the biological child you know it's going to be different, because it has different genes. So you'd think you couldn't affect its behaviour in quite the same way.'

'I'm not so sure. Think of Charlie. I tried to squash out any tendency towards violence when she was little, as you heard last night with the true tale of Tico. Not that Jeff's violence was necessarily genetic.'

'I know. But what a mistake that marriage was! Your father and I have often wondered what might've happened if we'd opposed it.'

'Nothing I expect, Mother. We would have gone ahead regardless. Or if you had succeeded there'd be no Charlie.' I sigh but not loudly enough for her to notice. I know my parents feel they were partly to blame for my marriage and she and I have had this conversation again and again.

'You were so headstrong you would have married anyway.' This facet of my teenage character provides them with the reassurance they need; it absolves them from feeling responsible for the failure of my marriage. And why should they? My mother is right; I was so crazy about Jeff I would have married him come what may. 'Anyway,' my mother continues, 'Charlie's loving and gentle.'

'Yes. So I don't quite see the logic of your argument about clones.'

'I think you do, Sally. You just told me that the differences between you and your clone arise through the environment. So you'd try to make the environment for your clone as different as possible to whatever you'd experienced, to avoid having the clone turn out like yourself!'

'Very clever,' I say. 'Maybe there's an argument for having the clone brought up elsewhere.'

'Is that the sort of thing you and Anthony talk about?'

I peek at my mother again. She looks innocently back and I burst out laughing. 'Even more clever than I thought! Are you asking if we discuss our work, or if we're going to reproduce? The answer's yes to the first and no to the second. We're not lovers either, if that's what you're getting at.'

'One should be cautious of course,' my mother says. 'But not too cautious. Now that reminds me, Sally, of what I intended to tell you about

Charlie. She wants to visit Jeff's grave, you know. She told me last night when you were on the phone.'

'Oh?'

'She's too frightened to tell you herself and she certainly won't ask you to take her.'

'I don't want to go.'

'That's as may be. But it would be better for her to go with you than anyone else. I asked Charlie if she missed her father. She said, 'The funny thing is, Gran, I don't. I've had a really happy life on my own with Mum.''

My eyes blur; I blink rapidly.

'She told me that she can't even remember much about him. So I said that she must remember something, that it would be a pity to let all her old memories of him lapse. She went quiet for a bit and then she said, 'I just remember games. Playing in the garden while he was digging, that sort of thing.' Then she said, 'It was really sad that he died so young,' and she asked me if weak hearts were genetic.'

'And what did you say?'

'That I didn't think so but that she should really speak to the resident geneticist. She asked me if there was anything else she should know about his death. The conversation was getting a bit beyond me, Sally. So I said that I couldn't remember the details — that's the thing about growing older, you find you actually can't — but I didn't think she needed to worry about the genetic aspect.'

My mother stops talking to take a quick look at her watch. 'Slower, Sally,' she says, as if she is talking to a cab driver. 'Plenty of time before my train.'

'No there isn't. What else did Charlie say?'

'Well, I could tell she thought I was being evasive. She must know that your father and I never thought that much of Jeff, although we've always tried to hide it. Then she said that not remembering much about him makes her feel quite guilty. It's as if she's betraying him by not remembering. After that, she burst into tears. That's why I came downstairs for another glass of wine when you were on the phone, Sally. It was for Charlie. I made her drink it to steady her nerves,' my mother says in her imitation of a Dame Edna Everage accent.

'I didn't notice.' A quick ingestion of alcohol has always been my mother's fix for an emotional outburst. Being tired and emotional comes before, not after, the drink in my mother's calculus. 'But I've been a bit preoccupied lately. I'm glad you've told me about this, Mum.'

'I thought you seemed rather distracted. But it was just as well last night that you were, because Charlie and I were able to have a really good heart-to-heart. I told her she's doing brilliantly and we're all so proud of her. But you might want to think about telling her more about Jeff, Sally. She's nearly grown up.'

'I know and I'm going to.' I have trouble keeping the anxiety out of my voice. 'It's a matter of choosing the right time.' But when? The days are flashing by too fast. 'I've only wanted to protect her.'

'And so you have, Sally. But there's such a

thing as being too cautious as I said to you earlier.'

'Not with respect to my driving.'

'There's a time and a place for everything,' says my mother.

And with that cryptic comment we arrive at Paddington Station. As we get out of the car, I hear the honking of birds.

'Is nowhere safe from Canada geese, not even Central London?' my mother says.

A flock of perhaps thirty of them is flying in spear-shaped formation above us.

30

THEN

'Look at that!' Jeff had one arm around my waist, and with his free hand he pointed east, to the triangle of geese flying in a tight formation, immediately above the dark smudge where the river met the pale sky.

'Going away, like us.' I ran my hand down his long back, and rested my head on his shoulder. We were standing on deck, about an hour into our honeymoon, delayed because the earliest ship we could book to La Spezia didn't leave until a month after our wedding.

We watched the geese wheel along the estuary, following its curves as if they were using the river as a navigational aid, until finally they were out of sight. Tilbury Dock was far behind us. The light was fading; the sky to the west was patterned improbably, like Venetian vellum, in swirls of pink and grey. As we watched, the clouds glowed before parting briefly, revealing the orange ball of the setting sun.

Jeff turned to me, and kissed me, a gentle salty kiss.

'Happy?'

'Never better.'

The ship had turned, so that we were facing eastwards again. An ashen full moon was now visible, advancing up the eastern sky as we watched, ripening visibly before assuming a warmer hue, and metamorphosing into a glowing golden disc. The air, smelling of salt with a faint odour of mud, was starting to feel damp as the evening quickened. A few seagulls flew alongside us, but their cries were all but drowned out by the throbbing of the ship's engines.

'Too dark to see much,' Jeff whispered into my ear.

In fact it was not, but I knew from the way he was nibbling my earlobe that he wanted to make love.

In our cabin Jeff turned on the desk-lamp, and we undressed each other in its yellow glow. The ship had begun to rock more, as we moved out into the Channel and away from the shelter of the land. When the ship lurched, we fell into the lower bunk.

I shut my eyes and felt the room moving.

That moment of love, that last moment of trust, was when Charlie was conceived. I am sure that was when Charlie was conceived. Our lovely child, our child of love; born just over nine months later.

For a long time we lay together on the bunk, not speaking.

'I'm crazy about you,' I said eventually, kissing his eyelids. Lightly I ran my forefinger along his profile, his high smooth forehead, his finely arched eyebrows, the straight nose.

'I'll always love you.' Jeff's voice was thick with emotion.

I ran my fingers through his blond hair, tousled after our love-making, and rested my head on his shoulder. In complete harmony we lay entwined on the bottom bunk, gently rocking with the movement of the ship. I was almost asleep when he said, 'Will you always love me?'

'Of course.' I turned my head to look into his clear green-gold eyes, a few centimetres away from mine, and raised my head to kiss him in the centre of his flawless forehead.

He grinned. A few minutes later, I slid off him, and out of the narrow bunk bed. I switched on the lamp over the small basin in the corner and washed. While I dressed, Jeff watched my every move with a calm unblinking gaze.

I had never felt happier.

Our two suitcases — wedding presents from Jeff's father — stood where they had been placed earlier, just inside the cabin door. I lifted the smaller one onto the desk and unzipped the fastening. I'd left our jumpers towards the top and we would need them before we went up on deck again. As I lifted the lid of the suitcase, a small flat object slid from on top of the clothes. I lunged to catch it but missed. It fell with a clatter on to the hard vinyl floor.

Jeff was out of bed in a flash, and at first I thought he was coming to help me. 'I'm sorry,' I said.

'That's not good enough.' His voice was cold.

There was a pause while he glared at me, his face red. Slowly he raised his right arm and slapped my face hard with the palm of his hand. Then with a deft wrist movement, he flicked his hand back and smacked my other cheek with the back of his hand.

I stood still, my cheeks ablaze with the blow and the humiliation, while Jeff bent down to pick up his iPod from the floor. He switched it on. The strains of his favourite Albinoni washed over us, peaceful music that was in sharp discord with the crashing of my heart and pounding of my head.

Jeff switched off his machine. He looked at me but said nothing. For a full minute we stared at each other. The red drained from his face while I waited for him to apologise. Finally, when his face had become a white mask, I left.

Blinded by tears now, I felt my way along the corridor and up onto the deck. I found a quiet spot at the back of the ship and clutched on to the handrail while I struggled to put Jeff's action into perspective. I felt as if I'd walked into icy water and was waiting for the numbness to set in, waiting for the moment when my body would take over so I wouldn't have to feel.

But it didn't come.

What was I going to do? 'Start as you mean to continue.' My mother said that to me the morning Jeff and I were married. I wished I could talk to her now but I'd never be able to tell her about this.

The coldness present in his voice when he said *that's not good enough*. He was like a different person. And the deliberation of his action. He had thought before he slapped me. It wasn't an act of passion. It was an act of punishment.

I should leave him. But how could I get off the ship? We were day one into a four-week holiday that my parents had paid for; our trip was their wedding gift. And what would I tell them if I could get off? I couldn't do it.

At least the iPod was OK. If it had broken I would have felt even worse. It would have complicated my already confused feelings. Jeff should have told me that he'd put it in there on top of the sweaters. It was more his fault than mine that it had fallen out. But why would he hit me for such a small thing? Could material possessions mean more to him than our love?

Certainly I would leave him if he didn't apologise. I could get off at the first port and make my way back to London.

I had to tell him he couldn't treat me like this.

For what seemed like hours I stood at the back of the boat, watching the night go by while I wondered what to do. The moon illuminated the wake of the ship so that it looked like a sheet of silver foil dragging along behind us. This incident might be like that wake, something that would be forever with us.

When shivering hit me, I began to pace up and down and a new thought struck me. Perhaps my face would be bruised; my skin marks easily. Maybe there would be finger marks on my cheeks, and someone might ask how that had happened. A bruise would be a real give-away. It would make it hard to protect him; to protect us.

But was I going to protect him? I'd married him for better and for worse. Shouldn't I give him another chance? Only if he apologised. I touched my face; it felt sore. I would have to creep back to our cabin and check. I didn't want to see Jeff, but perhaps he'd gone out too.

I returned quickly, hoping not to see anyone. The narrow corridors were strangely empty of people; the other passengers must be in their cabins or the bars. The lamps on the desk and over the hand basin were still glowing, but to my relief Jeff was not there. I looked in the mirror. My eyes were red-rimmed but my face wasn't bruised, not even a patch of red left on my cheeks. I washed my face with cold water, undressed and climbed into the top bunk. I pulled the covers right up over me, to blot out the world, to blot out my husband.

After some time Jeff returned. I was still awake, anxieties churning through my head, but I lay motionless with my back to the cabin.

'Sally,' he whispered.

I stayed where I was, eyes wide open. There was a smear of something on the wall in front of me. It looked like blood.

'Sally!' He touched my shoulder gently. 'I'm sorry, Sally darling. I really am.'

'Never do that again.' I rolled over and saw the lamplight reflected as circles in his lovely eyes. 'Never do it again or I'll leave you.'

'I love you Sal. I'm so sorry. Please forgive me.'

He put a box of chocolates in the bunk next to me. I ignored them, this guilt-offering. He leaned across and kissed my lips. And afterwards he took off his clothes and climbed into the top bunk with me.

31

NOW

We're going to be late for Jim's birthday party. This matters, I tell Charlie. The boat can't start on its odyssey from Little Venice until we're all there. She has spent half an hour changing from one set of black clothes to an almost identical set and that's why we're running late. She says that I don't really understand the subtleties of her wardrobe; she tells me that I shouldn't risk our lives by driving too fast down side roads, trying to save two minutes. I ignore her and focus on negotiating the car along the narrow streets.

Charlie is still sulking when we reach Little Venice, but I think she is nervous too at the prospect of seeing the beautiful Ben again. How could I have been so tactless as to suggest that all her clothes look the same, especially when she's always supportive of my appearance?

While Charlie slowly extricates herself from the car, I look over the canal below. The water is dark green and viscous. For the first time I notice that it seems to be flowing to the west; not the direction I would have predicted.

'You look lovely, Charlie,' I tell her when she's finally ready.

She smiles; she never sulks for long, only long enough to make her point. 'Flattery will get you everywhere,' she says. 'Like me to carry the bottle?'

After handing her the bag containing the wine and Jim's birthday card, I click my phone onto flight mode. We walk west along Maida Avenue to the Little Venice basin. The boat is going to take us east along the Grand Union Canal almost as far as Islington, before turning around and bringing us back again.

The weather has cleared, and a brisk wind is chasing away the last fragments of cloud from the washed blue sky and whipping the faded brown leaves from the plane trees. Kate is standing on the towpath next to a long dark green canal boat. It has smart yellow and red stripes along its gunwale and a brightly coloured design of flowers stencilled on the side of its long cabin. She is holding a clipboard and a pen; she looks as if she's enjoying the challenge of organising Jim's party, a project that would reduce lesser individuals to deep anxiety.

'Hello Sally! Hello Charlie! So glad you're here.' She grins happily and looks down at her clipboard, on which is a sheet of paper with a list of names 'Now we're only missing the Dhillons.' She puts a tick next to our names and guides us on board, squeezing my elbow as if she is especially pleased to see me.

At least thirty people are here already. There is a babble of voices. In the background, a barely discernible filament of music winds its way through the voices. We stand at the edge of the crowd waiting for something to happen.

'Sally!' Kate's husband, Jim, is shouting at me. I congratulate him on his birthday and introduce him to Charlie, who reminds us both that she has met him before. He is so tall that when I look up at him I can see how neatly he has clipped his nose hairs. There is a table of drinks behind him, with rows of glasses already filled. From this he picks up a glass of wine for me and for Charlie a glass of apple juice. 'Hope you like this stuff, Charlie,' he says. 'And I remember your mother likes white wine rather than red at lunchtime. When she drinks at all, that is.'

Charlie drifts off to find Ben. I take a sip of wine, and watch her flatten herself in an exaggerated way against the seats running the length of the cabin while she works her way through the crowd. She looks as if she's pretending to be a guerrilla trying to sneak unnoticed down a dangerous street. There is Ben next to the stereo player; with him is a boy of about the same age; he has frizzy hair that grows upwards, like mustard and cress. Ben is tall and blond, like Charlie, but with olive skin. When he sees Charlie, a wide smile lights up his sallow face with its strong beaked nose.

Jim is speaking to me but the noise in the cabin is so loud I have difficulty hearing what he is saying. I nod at what seem to be appropriate times and smile my good intentions. I think he is telling me something about how painful the age of forty is and that maybe he'll stay forever thirty-nine. Around us other people's words are skittering back and forth, competing with our exchange. When the Dhillons arrive and can find nothing suitable on the table of drinks, Jim shepherds them off to find some sparkling mineral water.

So here I am on my own, feeling detached, an alien in this boatload of earthlings, none of whom I know apart from our hosts, though I've been told that Clive and Martha are somewhere in the throng of people. Kate begins to instruct one of the boatmen to bring in the gangplank and cast us off. She then advises the other boatman to start the engine. There is something deeply engaging about her evident belief that this boat will never get moving without her assistance. Ropes are unfastened, the engine hums and thrums, and shortly we are moving off. The hubbub of voices dies down as people turn away from one another and move to the windows. The boat manoeuvres its way out of the basin and into the Grand Union Canal, past Zoë's block of flats, and through the brick tunnel under the Edgware Road. Soon people lose their interest in our stately progress along the canal and resume their conversations. The noise level is rising again, like the water in a lock.

Now Kate is at my side, saying, 'Follow me.' We weave through the crowd and climb up some steps to a little deck at the front. The wind has dropped and the sun feels warm on our faces.

Kate and I chat idly about work as we watch the passing scenery. Ahead of us is a metal bridge across which a train thunders. The sides of the bridge are decorated with graffiti — huge, flesh-pink lettering, rimmed in black, voluptuously splayed over the flat grey sides of the bridge. We float under Park Road, and on our right are the skeletons of trees, the few leaves still left on the branches fluttering like flags in the

183

breeze. The mosque lies beyond, and we're passing white stuccoed mansions, newly built.

After a while Kate vanishes inside. I should mingle too but the afternoon is so glorious I decide to stay outside a bit longer. Soon Charlie comes out on deck, with Ben and the other boy. We cruise past more people on the towpath, some strolling aimlessly, some marching purposefully; I listen to Charlie and the boys as they start telling stories about these people.

'There go the SMs,' Ben says as we glide past a couple in their twenties. The woman is wearing tight leather trousers that she might have been sewn into, a matching cropped jacket, and stiletto heeled black boots, and she's pulling along behind her a reluctant black poodle. The man with her is similarly dressed, only with black sneakers and no poodle.

'SMs?' Ben's friend enquires.

'Sado-masochists, Chris. She ties him up with her dog leash and beats him with the poodle.'

Ben and Charlie collapse into giggles. Chris is not amused; miffed no doubt at not knowing what SM means.

'See that toy boy there?' Ben points to a young man of about his own age. He's wearing a suit and slouching along with his hands in his trouser pockets. Beside him walks an elderly woman, probably his grandmother, with dyed blonde hair. I can see she's heavily made up, even across the couple of metres between the boat and the path, and she's wearing a pink suit with the skirt hemline well above her knees. Too short for someone of her age, it makes her legs look somehow vulnerable as if they might snap at any moment. She's being pulled along by an enthusiastic wolfhound. It seems that admission to the towpath is by leashed dog.

'There was a young toy-boy from Woy Woy,' Charlie says after we are out of earshot. 'Who saved up to purchase a borzoi.' She pauses.

'But she who had hired him, got jealous and fired him,' Ben contributes.

'So borzoi and toy boy lost employ!' says Charlie.

They crumple into another fit of giggles, while Chris smiles in a rather forced sort of way. I feel sorry for him: three is not a good number. Someone always feels left out.

'Very witty.' Kate has come out on deck unobserved and is standing right behind Ben. 'I've been looking all over for you, Ben.' Kate gives him a severe look. 'I want you to go inside and entertain your grandmother and Auntie Jean. They're sitting on their own.'

Ben makes a face at Charlie and Chris, and follows Kate into the cabin. It looks as if Chris and Charlie can think of nothing to say, so I ask Chris what he plans to do next year, after he leaves school. This sets him off on a long and complicated story about his preferences and his anticipated A-level grades, and how various combinations of results will lead to different outcomes, but that based on his performance to date the expected outcome is that he'll get into Cambridge. He speaks just like that, so I am not a bit surprised to learn that his parents are both statisticians.

The boat is now passing through the zoo, with the enormous aviary on our left. The netting is suspended from tall poles and looks too slack, as if it might blow in and entangle the birds. A seagull is perched on the top of a pole, on the outside, as if looking for an opportunity to get in. The sight of the waterfall running through the aviary sets Chris off again on another anecdote, this time an interesting one about the history of the three dams project in China. Charlie and Chris begin to converse quite animatedly. They are sweet and innocent, or am I being a romantic again?

32

THEN

I was a second-year undergraduate when Jeff and I decided to marry. We could never remember who thought of it first, but it seemed the natural thing to do. We both wanted a child, sooner rather than later.

'For God's sake, wait,' my mother said. 'You're far too young to marry. You're only nineteen.' I had rung her up to tell her the news. As soon as I heard her reaction I knew that this was a mistake; I should have told her face-to-face. I needed to be able to see her expression so I could better tailor my comments to suit her reaction.

'Twenty in one month's time.' I sat down on the floor of the white cube of our living room and contemplated Jeff's Patrick Heron forgery that adorned the far wall. He was very good at forging paintings; he could do almost any style but my favourite was this Patrick Heron, with its strong forms and primary colours.

'You're nineteen,' my mother said. 'Even if you were twenty, I'd still say you were far too young.'

'We're already living together.'

'I know, but that's different. Anyway, we never approved of that either, as you know. Wait a while. What's the hurry?'

'We're in love. You must have noticed.'

My mother made an uncharacteristic noise that could best be described as a snort, and there was a brief pause in the conversation. Then she said, 'Being in love's a delusion. Loving someone is not. When you're in love you're simply projecting your needs onto someone else.'

'You sound so cynical.'

'No; honest. Forget all the twaddle about being in love. Romantic love's simply a sexual gimmick. It ensures the reproduction of our species, or so I read recently in a book review.'

There was a silence that stretched and stretched. I felt surprised, not only by her cynicism or by the revelation that she had been following developments in socio-biology, but also because there was some truth in what she said. Romantic love as a sexual gimmick; that was a neat concept. Other animals didn't have this. Birds didn't have this, or not as far as we knew.

Yet Jeff was what I wanted and I was what he wanted. And anyway, you couldn't really take this socio-biology stuff seriously. I said, starting to giggle, 'Jeff and I were genetically programmed to fall in love with each other.'

She was not amused. 'You were genetically programmed to fall in love with *anyone*,' she said firmly. 'Jeff just happened to come along when your hormones were particularly rampant.'

I repressed a snigger at the thought of my rampant hormones and mentally filed my mother's comment away to tell Jeff later. 'I'm going to marry him anyway, Mum. You might as well get used to the idea. We'll do it with or without your approval. I've known him nearly two years, after all.'

'You'll change, Sally. You'll develop, both of you, and not necessarily in the same ways.' I could hear the thinly disguised irritation in her voice. 'He's not mature for his age. In some ways you're much more grown up than he is.'

Although tempted to ask her in what ways she thought Jeff was immature, I didn't want to get side-tracked again. 'We'll grow up together, Mum. Think of it that way.'

'Your father's not so keen on Jeff.'

I guessed this actually meant that she was not keen on Jeff. Apart from his family, my father was more or less indifferent to anyone who was not related to his work as a research chemist or who did not sail. As Jeff did neither, he had little hope of actively engaging his interest. 'Well, Dad's not marrying him,' I said. 'Anyway, fathers always think no man's good enough for their daughters.' I added, hoping to persuade her because of her own experience, 'Isn't that what Grandpa said to you when you got married? And you and Dad are very happy.'

'That was different,' she said, sighing. 'And you're our only child.'

'What's that got to do with anything? Jeff and I want to have a child. That's why we want to marry. Wouldn't you like to have a grandchild?' This was hitting below the belt; I knew there was nothing she would like more.

'But you're so young. Anyway, get Jeff to talk to your father. I'll have a word first, but I'm not at all keen on you doing this yet.'

It was the prospect of a grandchild that

clinched things. 'Thank you, Mum. You're the most wonderful woman in the world.'

'Humph,' she said, and hung up soon after.

The following weekend, Jeff and I went around to my parents' house. In old-fashioned style, Jeff and my father vanished into my father's study and emerged twenty minutes later, both looking somewhat embarrassed.

'It's OK,' Jeff said as they came out, and he gave my bottom a surreptitious pinch. 'He's agreed.'

'Your mother says the reception will be in our garden.' My father spoke these words as if he were reciting something learned by heart earlier. He then smiled at me in his absent-minded way before disappearing into his study again.

I married Jeff in late November.

A red-letter day.

33

NOW

The canal boat glides under an arched iron bridge. A tramp is lying on his side in the dirt under the bridge support, his face invisible behind his unkempt beard and hair. He has wrapped some newspapers around him, as if even this mild autumn afternoon is too cold. The contrast between us and him seems almost obscene. I start when I hear a deep male voice behind me. 'You're in the biology department, aren't you?'

Two men are standing behind me. One is taller than the other but apart from that they're virtually indistinguishable, dressed as they are in almost identical tweed jackets and corduroy trousers. Charlie and Chris are so intent on their conversation they don't notice the new arrivals.

'Frank McDonald,' says one of the tweed jackets. 'And this is John Smythe. Kate said we should come out and introduce ourselves. We're in the sociology department.'

How like Kate to take action to ensure I'm not a wallflower. I look over the shoulders of the tweed jackets and see her waving at me from inside the cabin. I grin and wave back, before shaking hands with each of the tweed jackets. I find I cannot remember which is which.

'I'm sure I've seen you before. Some conference

I expect,' says the tall tweed jacket with the resonant voice.

'Senate, more likely,' says the short tweed jacket.

'Yes, of course,' I say. Senate is full of men like these.

'Kate tells me you're a very good friend of Zoë McIntyre,' says the tall tweed jacket.

I don't say anything. There is a pause while the short tweed jacket struggles to think who Zoë McIntyre is. Then in tones of incredulity: 'The woman who does that TV show?'

'Yes. Kate says you've known each other for years, Sally. School, I think she said. Or was it university.' I am about to say that we haven't known each other quite that long but I don't get a chance. 'Zoë was the presenter for *Rearranging Lives*,' the tall tweed jacket explains to his friend. 'Do you remember that TV programme years ago? I used to have a crush on her.'

'I don't watch much TV,' says the short tweed jacket with a sigh, as if watching TV is a hobby that he might engage in if only he had a bit more time.

'That was the show where she put someone doing one job into a totally different job at another firm, and watched how they coped with it.'

'Ahh, I remember now. They used hidden cameras to record colleagues' reactions.'

'Zoë was the good-looking one who did the story. I always thought the data from that would make a nice case study. In fact I tried to contact her a couple of times about that but she never replied.'

'You'd have trouble getting that sort of thing past an ethics committee these days,' says the short tweed jacket. 'I thought the programme was rather ghastly, if you want to know.' He is right; it was. I watched one episode after I met Zoë and that was enough.

'It was hilarious actually,' says the tall tweed jacket. 'But there was some scandal when she was doing that. She got beaten up or something, it was all over the papers. She appeared on her programme with a black eye.'

I freeze. Opening my mouth to speak, I can only manage a strangled mumble, but neither tweed jacket takes any notice.

'There was going to be a court case,' the taller tweed jacket continues, in quieter tones now. I am relieved that Charlie and Chris have their backs to us and won't hear this conversation.

'I remember now. They caught the chap who did it. He was her *lover* apparently.' It's obvious that the short tweed jacket is not used to saying the word lover; it's as if he has put it in inverted commas to emphasise that it's a word he doesn't usually use.

'He died in mysterious circumstances a few days later.'

'Well, that bit passed right by me,' says the short tweed jacket.

'I'm an avid reader of that sort of thing. Living vicariously.' They both laugh.

Charlie turns round at this point. I pray that she hasn't heard but she fixes her green eyes on the taller tweed jacket. He looks at her as if she is a specimen from another tribe that he's encountered for the first time. She says, 'When was that?'

'It was only some silly gossip about Zoë.' A pulse is pounding in my throat. I glare at the tweed jacket but he is looking at Charlie not me.

'When did Zoë get beaten up?' Charlie says again.

The tweed jacket will never be able to remember this and I begin to relax slightly. But he pulls at his chin for a bit as if that will aid his memory and eventually says, 'I reckon it was about ten years ago. I remember seeing the head-lines on the way to the cricket the year England played Pakistan. I went with you, Frank, do you remember?'

'Was that in London?' My daughter's voice is sharp.

The short tweed jacket says, 'It was at The Oval. I remember the cricket but I can't recall seeing the headlines on the way. I only went to one test in that series. I couldn't afford to take off any more time then and I can't afford to now.'

'I guess you wouldn't have been following the cricket back then,' the tall tweed jacket says to Charlie, before beginning to laugh like a department store Santa Claus, ho-ho-ho.

'I guess not.' Charlie's voice is unfriendly and her brow furrowed. She turns her back to us and rests her elbows on the planking across the prow of the boat, with her chin cupped in her hands. Next to her Chris is still talking, as if there's been no interruption.

My heart is beating too hard and my palms feel sticky. Charlie will ask questions soon; I shall have to tell her what really happened. In the meantime I listen to the tweed jackets talk on and on about cricket.

Kate taps me on my shoulder. 'Would you like something to eat?'

'Thanks. I'll come in and get it.'

'You stay here. Mind a place for me,' she says, grinning. 'Spread yourself out a bit.'

I watch her as she ducks down the steps next to the two tweed jackets, and fights her way back through the bodies to where the food and drinks are laid out at the far end of the cabin. Chris soon decides to follow her example and vanishes into the cabin. I wink at Charlie. 'Having a good time?'

'Yeah,' she responds like an automaton. She is looking perturbed, a frown creasing her brow. 'Mum, you didn't tell me Zoë had been bashed up. Those two guys were talking about it just now.'

I look at the tweed jackets, who are now arguing about the European Union. 'That was years ago.' This is not the place to talk to Charlie about Zoë. 'I'd forgotten all about it.'

'What happened?'

'I can't remember the details.' She can tell when I'm lying so I avert my face and focus on the shore.

'I'll ask Zoë.'

'Don't do that. It was too long ago.' I look Charlie in the eye. 'It's best forgotten, Charlie. Zoë wants to put it behind her.'

'It *is* behind her, Mum. Well behind her. So I can ask her about it next time I see her.'

'No, you mustn't do that.' I half shut my eyes at her. This is my way of signalling that we can't discuss the matter here, not with the tweed jackets nearby. They might be arguing about the European Union but it's possible they can do two things at once, talk and listen, and they clearly love a bit of gossip, especially the taller one. 'I'll tell you later, I promise. Enjoy the day, Charlie. It's such lovely weather.' Please, please, Charlie, I think. Please not here. Not now, not today. Not in front of everyone. Tomorrow I'll tell you the truth. Tomorrow, when we're at home and no one is listening, I'll tell you what happened.

She gazes at me; the iris of her eyes the exact same green as her father's. Her face seems paler today: perhaps that's the light washing over her skin that's so fine you'd need a magnifying glass to see the pores. I tell her, 'Let's not spoil today by dragging up the past. Not yet. Wait a bit. I'll tell you later.' I turn away from her, back to the tweed jackets.

Chris and Ben return laden with food. They've brought some for the tweed jackets and me as well. At Kate's behest, Ben explains; she's caught up with relatives inside. Charlie seems distracted and makes only a slight effort when the two boys resume the game of inventing lives for the people strolling along the towpath. Chris and Ben are showing off for Charlie's benefit but she isn't taking much notice. Soon she abandons all pretence of joining in, and stares at the water as it slips by, as if that will provide the answer to everything.

We are now puttering past white-painted warehouses with balconies overlooking the canal.

The boat slows as we approach the twin locks at Hampstead Road. One of the boatmen jumps ashore and winches open the gates to the lock on the left of the canal, and we drift into the coffin-shaped enclosure. I watch the rows of wet bricks lining the sides of the lock as the boat descends with the escaping water. In a few minutes we drop several metres, and the pit in which the boat is floating fills with the stench of diesel fumes. Tomorrow I'll have to tell Charlie the truth and the prospect sickens me.

When we reach the lower level of the canal, the fargates to the lock are winched open and the boat moves out into a wide basin of water. How am I going to find the words to tell Charlie? I feel a deep foreboding. She will hate me for this. The trust she has in me will be broken.

It's a relief when Charlie and the boys disappear inside to fetch some more food, leaving me with a plate of largely untouched sandwiches and the two tweed jackets. The boat manoeuvres slowly around the basin, and I find myself face-to-face with a woman on the shore. She is slightly younger than me and is sitting with two men on the canal-side.

'Give us something to eat,' she says. She has an Irish accent.

Before I can say anything she leans over and picks up the plate of sandwiches from the decking in front of me. Her action is faultlessly timed — as soon as she has the plate in her hand the boat swings away, and I hear her laughter ring out as the distance between us widens. I join the tweed jackets in laughing too, and one of them offers me his last samosa. The woman with my sandwiches and her two companions salute as the boat reverses round and we go back into the lock again.

Behind the woman with my sandwiches is a warehouse building painted blue and grey, with a saw-toothed roof. Each gable of the roof is crenulated, and on the top-most crenulation sits a large eggcup, painted blue and white and containing a plaster egg. The whole scene looks so surreal that I might be dreaming. But I hear the tweed jackets continuing their discourse as if nothing has happened and I know that this is reality. After a while Kate joins us again, together with Clive and Martha from my department; our conversation flows with the boat all the way back to Little Venice.

Charlie is sitting inside with Ben and Chris on the bench seat running the length of the cabin. Through the window behind them I catch a glimpse of my car parked high above us, and there beyond is the red mansion block of flats in which Zoë lives. We slip under the road bridge and back into the basin. A few ducks swim sedately out of our way, unhurried, as if they are big enough to induce our boat to change course if there is any danger of a collision.

The boatman throws a rope over a capstan, and we are secured to land once more. People are gathering together their possessions and preparing to disembark.

I sit down next to Charlie. 'The boys have gone to find their coats,' she says. She is radiant now, as if she has forgotten all about Zoë. 'Ben's asked me out,' she whispers. 'To a party in two weeks' time.' I look at her glowing face. In her delight she's forgotten all about our earlier conversation with the tweed jackets.

Kate and Jim are already off the boat and standing on the towpath. I hug each of them; they look so happy and right together. Charlie and I make our departure, leaving most of the other guests still milling around Little Venice basin with their last minute conversations and farewells.

When we reach the car, Charlie says, 'Can you drop me at your college library on the way home, Mum? I want to look up something for an assignment.'

'Can't it wait?'

'I want to get it out of the way.'

'Have you got your bus pass?'

Charlie pulls it out of her pocket, together with a crumpled ten pound note. 'Always prepared.'

'Have you got your mobile?'

'You rushed me out of the house so fast I forgot to pick it up. I haven't got my keys either.'

After unlocking the glove compartment of the car, I hand Charlie the bunch of keys kept there for emergencies. 'Take these,' I tell her. 'I'll go to the supermarket while you're at the library.'

I start the engine and pull cautiously out into the street. Charlie says nothing on the drive to Gower Street and I'm glad of it. What will I tell her tomorrow — or maybe tonight — when she brings up the topic of Zoë? Her joy at being asked out by Ben will buy me only so much time.

There's nowhere to park in front of the college library but Charlie leaps out when I slow down. 'See you,' she says before she dashes between parked cars. I blow her a kiss but she doesn't look back, and I feel a splinter of hurt. The car behind me honks and I continue on, one small car in the steady stream of Saturday evening traffic.

34

NOW

The house is in darkness; Charlie can't be home yet. The phone starts ringing as I'm locking up my car. It rings in stereo from the extension in the living room and the one in the dining room below. Picking up my canvas bags full of shopping, three in each hand, I stagger up the steps to our front door. Twelve peals before the answering machine kicks in and eight have gone by the time I unlock the front door. Dumping the bags on the hall floor, I race for the extension, reaching it on the eleventh ring.

'Hello?' One of my bags falls sideways, spewing its contents onto the polished wooden floorboards.

'Sally! Sally, I've just arrived at Heathrow airport,' Anthony says.

'Heathrow?' My voice sounds breathless, and this is not only from racing up the steps with the heavy shopping bags. 'Anthony, are you here in England?'

'Yes, I've just got in. Didn't you get my message?'

'What message?' I look at the answering machine and see that there are three waiting. 'I didn't check when I got back from the boat trip. But how lovely that you're in London!'

'I woke up this morning and wanted to see

201

you. So I called the airline and managed to get a seat. I knew you'd be home tonight and tomorrow. You told me last Thursday when we spoke.'

Overcome, unable to speak a word, I stand like a teenager smiling at the wall.

'Is that OK, Sally? I do hope you don't mind.'

'Anthony, I'm delighted. Really delighted. Are you coming here now?'

'Yes. I'll get the express train to Paddington, there's one leaving in a few minutes. I'll drop my bag off at my flat first and take a cab from there over to your place. I should reach you by about half-past nine.'

I look at my watch. It's a few minutes past eight o'clock.

'I'll hold supper for you.'

'Are you sure that's all right?'

'Yes. And it's more than all right. It's wonderful.'

After hanging up, I look at my reflection in the mirror over the fireplace: I look radiant, I look years younger.

I key in the digits for the phone's message bank. The first message is from Charlie's friend Amrita telling Charlie to meet her at Belsize Park Tube station at half-past eight tonight. I suppose Charlie has already been home and heard this, and saved it as message unheard as a way of letting me know what she's up to. Odd that she hasn't left a note though; she usually leaves details of where she's going on the pad by the telephone. Next there's a brief message from my mother, followed by one from Anthony. He phoned from Logan airport; I can hear flight announcements in the background. His flight is about to depart; he's made a spur of the moment decision, he says, to fly to London for a few days, and hopes I might see him. The impulsiveness of his action is in stark contrast to the careful, reserved way he gives his message. Perhaps he thought I mightn't be pleased. But pleased cannot describe the emotions I am feeling: I alternate between excitement and nervousness, and relief that there's enough food in my shopping bags to cook a good meal.

After pulling my mobile phone out from the depths of my handbag, I switch it off flight mode. It pings a few seconds later with another message from Anthony at Logan airport, the duplicate of the one he left on the landline. There is nothing from Charlie though. Leaving the phone on the bench, I race around the kitchen, putting the groceries away. Afterwards I inspect the rest of the house. It doesn't look too bad. The cleaner came on Friday; we always tidy up before she comes, and we haven't yet had time to reduce it to the chaotic level that we reach by mid-week. I put on a CD of Vengerov playing Prokofiev's first violin concerto, and begin to prepare supper.

We shall have pasta with broccoli sauce and green salad. I make up the sauce, mixing the broccoli with crème fraîche, braised garlic and anchovies, and set this mixture aside while I prepare the salad. Though the scherzo movement of the concerto makes me feel agitated, it is followed by the lyrical and calming third movement. After putting a bottle of white wine in the freezer to chill rapidly, I fill a large pan with water and set it on the hob ready to turn on when Anthony arrives.

Next I have a quick shower and change into jeans, a navy blue cable-knit sweater, and my brown Hobbs loafers. The phone rings while I'm running wet fingers through my hair to restore the curl.

'Is Charlie there?' Amrita says. 'We were supposed to meet at Belsize Park Tube unless she called me back to say otherwise. But she hasn't turned up.'

'Really? I thought she must have come home and gone out again to meet you.' I look at my watch. It's just after nine o'clock and Charlie doesn't have her mobile phone with her so I can't call her.

'I'm sure she'll turn up soon,' says Amrita. 'We're going to have to go in now; the film's about to start.'

'I expect she got carried away at the library,' I say. 'She'll probably arrive home any minute.'

But I'm worried. I dropped Charlie off at five o'clock. Suppose it took her longer than two hours in the library, say three hours. And it would take her another hour to get home. That brings us to around nine o'clock. She should be here shortly. If not, surely she would have called me. She is usually really reliable like that; although maybe she tried to and was unable to find a public phone. They are few and far between in this mobile phone age and some of them require a credit card rather than cash.

Charlie keeps a list of her friends' telephone numbers on the bench next to the kitchen phone. I try calling a few of them without luck; her friends are either out themselves or don't know where Charlie is. The last parent I speak to thinks I'm panicking unnecessarily. Charlie has probably run into some friends and gone to the pub, he suggests, and intimates that I'm over-reacting.

'Charlie always tells me where she is,' I explain. He promises that his daughter Lindsay will let me know on her return whether or not she's seen my daughter.

It is now nine-fifteen. I pick up my mobile phone, put on a jacket and a scarf, and go out into the street. All is quiet; cars are parked up and down the road but there is no through traffic tonight. No one is coming, no one is going; we might be in a village rather than in a huge city. I wander aimlessly around, unsure of what I'm doing out here. I don't want to range too far away: I have to be able to hear our landline ring in case Charlie calls that instead of my mobile.

At nine-thirty I go inside again and check the answering machine. No more messages. Although Anthony was the last person to call, I dial the call recall service, in case the phone rang while I was in the street and I didn't hear it. The automated operator tells me that I was called today at 20.07 and that the caller withheld their number. That would have been Anthony phoning from his mobile or from one of those rare items, a public phone, at Heathrow.

When I hear a car pull up in the street, I dash to the window. Anthony is climbing out of a black cab. I run to open the front door. He is carrying a bunch of red roses but he doesn't have time to do anything with these because I throw my arms around his neck.

'Anthony, how wonderful to see you!' I would almost certainly not be hugging him like this were it not for the fact that a part of my brain — the cautious reserved part — has been shut down by my anxiety about Charlie.

I bury my face in Anthony's chest. He is taller than I remembered. His chest smells of clean skin and wool. The reason he smells so good, I remind myself, is that his genetically produced immunological attributes are quite different to mine. This is why his scent is just right. No other reason. He runs his free hand over my upper back before lifting my chin and kissing me gently. I push the front door shut with my foot, and he kisses me again; and for a few moments I forget everything.

We are interrupted by the phone ringing. Charlie's friend Lindsay has just got my message. She hasn't seen Charlie, she says, but will call back if she hears anything. 'I'm sure she's fine,' Lindsay says.

My anxiety is increasing. I try ringing Zoë's landline. Charlie does have Zoë's keys on the big bunch that I gave her when I dropped her at the library, and she might have gone to her flat on some whim. I hold my breath as the phone rings on and on. No one picks up and the answering machine doesn't click on. After a number of rings I'm automatically disconnected. Then I remember that Zoë is off somewhere, Amsterdam probably,

I wish I'd listened more carefully when we last spoke. When I call her mobile number the recorded message clicks in at once: she either has the phone switched off or she's out of range. I leave a message asking her to ring me when she can.

Anthony and I sit in the living room. We occupy armchairs opposite each other, separated by the coffee table on which I placed a vase containing the long-stemmed red roses. Through the glass surface of the coffee table I see his long legs stretched out. His feet are a few centimetres away from mine. I focus on his slightly scuffed brown shoes while I begin to tell him of my fears. After I finish, I look up. His expression is intense, his eyebrows lowered in concentration. He runs me through the afternoon again: what was the time when Charlie and I left the canal boat, what was the time when I dropped Charlie off at the library.

'When does the library shut?' he asks, when I pause for breath.

'Nine-thirty.' In the excitement of the last couple of hours I forgot this. The time is now one minute before ten o'clock. 'It's too late to phone the college.'

'If Charlie stayed there until it closed, forgetting the time, she might've only just left.' Anthony says.

'Yes.' I feel slightly cheered by this.

'So she should be back shortly; by ten-thirty at the very latest.'

'Perhaps we should eat. You must be hungry and tired.'

'Hungry, yes. Tired, no. I'm on US time, five

207

hours behind here. So it's five o'clock in the afternoon for me. I can party all night if you'd like to.'

'When do you have to go back?'

'Monday.'

We have nearly two whole days.

We go downstairs to the kitchen, and I put the pasta on to cook while Anthony tells me of his experiences in the United States. The funny bits I can laugh at, it doesn't take much energy to smile. But when he asks about my research project, I find my mind has been erased clean of sensible thoughts about work let alone the ability to talk about it. 'The medical testing,' he prompts, 'you're introducing *Helicobacter pylori* into artificially induced stomach tissue, aren't you?'

I stand still and wonder where I put the wine. 'I can't concentrate, Anthony.' Thoughts spin around my head, bright flashes of hope followed by darker streaks of despair.

'Let me pour you a drink.'

At this point I remember that the bottle of wine is in the freezer. I left it too long; it's icy cold. Anthony takes it from me and starts opening cupboards at random.

'Glasses ready on the bench,' I say automatically. He pours the wine and hands me a glass.

'To us,' he says. We clink glasses. I resolve to drink only a little in case I have to go out in my car to collect Charlie from somewhere.

By half-past ten Charlie is still not home and Anthony and I eat the pasta. It is overcooked. Anthony chats vivaciously over supper, trying to

208

distract me from my worries. By eleven o'clock she is still not here, and Anthony is looking uneasy too.

'I'd better phone the hospitals,' I say. 'Just in case.'

'Would you like me to do it?'

'No. They might want a detailed description and you've never met her.'

I call up the accident and emergency unit at the Royal Free Hospital. My hand is shaking so much I key in the wrong number and have to try again. No one has come in fitting Charlie's particulars. Next I try University College Hospital and there is no news there either. I find my fingernails are digging into my palms. I tell myself that no news is good news.

Anthony and I clean up the kitchen. I try not to imagine what might have happened to Charlie, but crisp images keep coming unbidden to my mind, as if someone is showing me one of those old canisters of photographic slides. Round and round they go in the projector, round and round in my head. Charlie is prostrate on the side of a canal; Charlie is floating face down in the Thames; Charlie is lying beaten or worse in a back alley near Kings Cross Station; Charlie is wandering with amnesia through the streets of London, unable to remember her way home. Round and round the images go, clear and sharp. See them once, see them again. Gritty black and white photo-realism. Newspaper images of other people's lives.

I try to pull myself together. Anthony loads the dishwasher. After putting cling film over

Charlie's meal, I place it in the refrigerator, and wipe down the benches. I make a pot of tea and we take it and some cups up to the living room.

It's half-past eleven and still no sign of Charlie. Anthony hits on the idea of playing Scrabble to keep us occupied while we are waiting. Waiting for Charlie. Waiting for her return; waiting for some news. I get out the Scrabble board and we begin a game. The minutes pass by, the quarter-hours pass by; we hear the old clock in the dining room ringing them out.

Anthony is a competitive player and so am I, even now. It's almost as if I am playing a game with fate. If I can win at Scrabble my daughter will come home safely; if I lose she will never return. I don't mention this stupid fantasy to Anthony in case he thinks I am a bad loser. Maybe later, if I win and Charlie comes home, I will tell him. Maybe later we can laugh at all of this.

Anthony puts down on the board the word 'lover', building on a word of mine. I have an S at the ready, and construct the word 'syntax' from Anthony's contribution, thereby turning the 'lover' into 'lovers'. I look up at Anthony and hold his glance. We would have become lovers tonight if Charlie had not gone missing. We say nothing; we continue with our contest, our way of filling in the time.

Towards the end of the game Anthony puts down on the board the word 'crasis'. I challenge him on this, and tell him it's a waste of two tiles containing the valuable letter S.

'You're a biologist, you should know what crasis means,' he says, laughing. He is parodying what I said the time we visited Tate Modern when I teased him for not knowing what a banksia was. Funny to think that our lunch together and trip to Tate Modern was the first time, the only time, we have been out together, and yet I feel as if I've known him for years.

'Are you listening, Sally?' Anthony's hand is on my arm. 'Crasis means a combination of elements or qualities in animals' bodies. As well as something like a diphthong.'

'I don't believe you,' I say. 'You're making it up.' Opening the iPad I keep on the coffee table, I click on the dictionary app to look up 'crasis' and find that Anthony is right.

'You're showing off,' I say. But I know he is trying to make me laugh, and he has succeeded.

I win the game. Charlie will come home. Anthony's crasis has helped, for I am able to use the last S as an ending for a seven-letter word that brings me bonus points. I have won. Crasis. Crisis: that is what we are having tonight. A crisis.

While Anthony is preparing the Scrabble board for another game, I go out into the street. For a few moments I stand in front of our place, hoping that Charlie will turn up now that I've come out to meet her. But there is no sign of life. Trafalgar Terrace is in darkness, save for yellow-orange pools of light from the street lamps. Ours is in the middle of the terrace of houses lining this short street. The other houses are in darkness, or display faint rectangles of light diffused through drawn curtains. But our uncurtained windows are ablaze, as if we are throwing a party.

Shivering, I go inside and run upstairs to look in Charlie's room. Perhaps she has crept in while we were playing Scrabble, perhaps I shall find her asleep in her bed.

I switch on her light and find the room is empty. The bed is still made, the curtains are not drawn. I peer out of her window at the night. There is a crescent moon and the sky glows a dull orange, as it always does in London from the sodium street lights. There are patches of yellow light on the narrow strip of back garden, from the window where I am standing and from the living room below. I draw the curtains, and glance again at my watch. One o'clock on Sunday morning.

I run downstairs and find Anthony standing at the front bay window, looking out. He turns as I enter the room, and holds out an arm for me. We stand side-by-side surveying the quiet street.

'Still no sign,' he says. 'Let's start a new game. It can't be too much longer now.'

I can think of nothing to say. 'It can't be too much longer,' he said. Not that *Charlie* can't be too much longer. *It* can't be too much longer. It can't be too much longer before a policeman is knocking at the door.

We begin our second game of Scrabble. Time passes. I find it hard to concentrate and make silly moves. Anthony is no better, although I suspect that he's humouring me. I interrupt the game to call the accident and emergency units a couple of times, but they know nothing. The night is wearing on, and I fear that I'll never see my daughter alive again.

35

NOW

There is a crash as the roof shatters. The room is pitch-black and I don't know where I am. Though I'm sitting on the edge of a bed, I don't know where it's located. I stand up, and walk carefully to where I think the door is. Holding my arms up in front of me, I grope for the door handle. But there is no door here, only walls, smooth plastered walls. I am shut in, I am incarcerated here, and there is no way out. And I have lost something, something important; I have lost the keys. My heart is banging in my chest and a wave of panic drowns out all rationality. I am a primitive woman buried alive in her cave. Screaming, I bang on the wall with my fists. Then my right hand touches something smooth and warmer than the walls: it's a piece of plastic, it's a plastic switch. I flick it and a bright light fills the room, momentarily blinding me.

I am standing in the living room of my house in Kentish Town. Everything is in its proper place. Look, there next to the light switch is the doorpost. Groping in the dark I had missed it completely. Dripping with sweat, I look at my watch. Three o'clock in the morning.

Now it all comes flooding back. Charlie is missing. And Anthony is not here either.

Next I hear footsteps on the stairs. It's

Anthony, running up from the kitchen.

'Are you OK?' he asks. 'I heard screaming.'

'Is she home?'

'No, Sally. Not yet. There's no news yet.' He puts his arms around me and hugs me; then he leads me back to the sofa. We sit down side by side.

'I had a dream,' I say.

'Tell me about it.'

I recount my dream. It was a variant of the usual. It was a dream about Charlie, about Charlie ten years ago when she was only seven years old. In this dream we were in a beautiful room at the top of a round tower, in a fairy-tale castle. Over our heads rose a high glass dome, through which could be seen a sprinkling of stars and a thin sickle moon that had faintly illuminated Charlie's face. Suddenly there was a loud explosion, the glass roof cracked and splintered. And Charlie vanished, just like that. She vanished. The room was thrown into darkness, the stars and the moon had gone. And Charlie was no more. Gone in a crash of glass; a shattering sprinkling of glass.

At this moment I hear sounds from the street. A car pulls up outside the house, a car door opens and a few seconds later slams shut. It's the police; it must be the police, coming to tell me what has happened.

36

NOW

Flinging open the front door, I almost fall on top of Charlie, hand extended about to insert the key into the lock. Over her shoulder, I see in the street below, not a police car but a black London cab.

'Thank God you're here.' I throw my arms around her neck and give her a big hug. When she doesn't respond, I hold her at arm's length; she looks pale apart from the dark smudges under her eyes. 'Are you OK, Charlie? I've been worried sick about you.'

'Yeah,' she says. 'I'll explain in a minute. I need eleven squids for the cab driver.'

I get my handbag from the newel post of the stair, where it always hangs when I'm at home, and accompany Charlie out to the cab. I lean through the window. The driver is a dark middle-aged man and his cab reeks of aftershave and disinfectant. I give him two notes, a tenner and a fiver. 'Keep the change,' I tell him. He nods and drives off quickly, in case I change my mind.

'That's much too big a tip.' Charlie's voice is cross.

'Money's the least of my worries right now. And he did bring you home.'

'That's what the eleven pounds was for.'

We glare at each other under the orange streetlight. 'You've got a lot of explaining to do, young woman,' I tell her.

'So have you.' Charlie strides up the steps to our front door. The heels of her Doc Martens are scuffed. I follow her and shut the door behind us, rather too hard; we stand face-to-face in the hall.

'Where have you been, Charlie?'

'At Zoë's flat.' Charlie's eyes will not meet mine but dart around the hall as if she is trying to find something more interesting.

'I tried calling there about ten o'clock but there was no answer.'

'Well, I wasn't going to pick up the phone, was I? Like, get real, Mum, I wasn't even supposed to be there!'

'But why didn't you call me? You must have known I'd be sick with worry.' My relief mingles with fatigue that washes over me like a tidal wave. My legs give way and I subside onto the second step of the staircase. Charlie is home, I tell myself, that is the main thing. I must be calm; we must avoid a row; we are both too tired.

And there is Anthony waiting in the living room.

'Don't you start asking me why I haven't done things,' Charlie shouts in an uncharacteristic burst of anger. 'This is your fault, you know, this whole thing is your fucking fault!'

'How is that?' My voice is icy cold, as if I can calm Charlie's anger. 'And don't swear at me, Charlie. I don't like it.'

'You fucking didn't tell me! You've never told me anything.'

'Like what?' I stand up again and clutch the newel post.

'You lied to me. You said Dad died of a heart attack but he didn't. He banged his head when he was doped up with drugs and alcohol and died of a haematoma. Whatever the fuck that is.'

Charlie's voice reverberates around the stairwell and over these echoes I hear the blood pounding in my ears. I should have been the one to explain to her exactly how Jeff died. She's learned about her father but not from me. Without thinking I open my mouth. 'I can tell you what a haematoma is.' It's an effort to keep my voice unruffled. 'It's bleeding between the brain and the skull. It puts pressure on the brain.'

'My mother, the fucking scientist. You always have a pat answer for everything.'

'Not now, Charlie. Let's not have a row. Why don't we go upstairs and talk about it quietly.'

'And Dad beat you up too, just like he did Zoë.' Charlie shouts out these words, my calmness enraging rather than comforting her.

'What gives you that idea?' I half-shut my eyes and frown at her.

'What do you think? I read it in newspapers in your college library. That's what I was doing, checking through old papers on microfiche. The *Guardian* and *The Times*, in the year Dad died. Does that mean anything to you? What those blokes on the boat said was pretty useful. I know enough about cricket to work out when that test series must have taken place and that it seemed to coincide roughly with Dad's death. And do you know why I had to do it that way? Because you couldn't fucking bring yourself to tell me what happened!'

I look at the floorboards while wondering what to say. I should have told her about this long ago; instead of pretending to myself I was waiting for the right moment. 'I'm sorry, Charlie. I'm really sorry,' I cannot think of anything more to add. This is too sudden, too soon. And I cannot speak of this with Anthony listening.

'I asked you what had happened to Zoë, didn't I, Mum? Like, I asked you on the boat and you couldn't tell me.'

'Do you think I could begin to tell you what happened in front of a boat load of near-strangers?'

'You could've said *ask me later*, couldn't you?'

'I kind of did, Charlie. Don't you remember? I said I'd talk to you later.' My voice sounds too reasonable, possibly even patronising. Yet this rationality is not what I am feeling. I want to hug Charlie. I want to explain everything to her, but not with Anthony standing in the room next to us.

My apparent calmness inflames Charlie's anger again. She takes a step towards me and I think of Jeff. Charlie is Jeff's child; sometimes I forget that Charlie is Jeff's child too. I flinch and turn my head to one side. Shutting my eyes, I wait for her to deliver a physical blow.

'Open your eyes and look at me, Mum,' Charlie says, more quietly now. 'You can't tell the truth about anything, can you?' Her eyes appear emerald green against the flushed red of her skin. She thinks I've betrayed her trust. She has a right to be angry. I should have told her something of my past. Our past. She continues, more calmly although her voice is clear and carrying: 'You've hidden your boyfriends from me. You've never brought them home, your toy boys that Zoë's told me about. Use them then lose them!'

'I know you're very upset, Charlie.' I find it hard to speak; my mouth is dry and my voice shaking, and only by carefully enunciating each word can I marshal my thoughts. 'But now you're being silly.'

'Not as silly as you've been,' Charlie says. The worst of her anger is over, and I can see her eyes filling with tears. For the first time since getting home she looks into the living room and sees the Scrabble game spread out on the coffee table. And there is Anthony standing with his back to us looking out of the front bay window. No way out for him, Charlie and I are blocking the exit. His whole body language expresses discretion.

'Who's that?' she hisses.

'Anthony.'

'The Blake bloke,' says Charlie loudly. 'The clone drone. Trapped in the living room. He knows all our little secrets now.'

Anthony turns, right on cue, and walks towards us. His face is a mask that reveals nothing. There is no trace of embarrassment, no sign of awkwardness. 'Charlie, how nice to meet you,' he says, as if they have been introduced at some drinks party. 'Anthony Blake,' he adds.

'I've met you,' says Charlie, glowering. 'On the phone. Doesn't that count? The countless times the clone drone's phoned.'

Anthony ignores her rudeness and puts out his hand as if to shake hers. For some reason she finds this comical and bursts into hysterical laughter. Anthony appears unfazed however. But Charlie doesn't shake his hand.

'Your mother's been frantic with worry. I'm so glad you're safe.' He looks at me and smiles. 'I think I'll make some tea.' He clatters noisily down the stairs to the kitchen. Glad to get away, I expect.

'That was incredibly rude, Charlie,' I say, when Anthony is out of earshot.

'Who cares?' she says, scuffing her boot on the wooden floorboards. 'Like, I'm fed up with all this pretence.'

I hold out my arms to her but she pushes past me and races up the stairs two at a time. As she passes I catch a faint whiff of spirits on her breath; Zoë's cognac, I suppose. Next I hear her bedroom door slam.

I look at my watch. Half three. This will get rid of Anthony. This will remove him from my life. Like my toy boys, as Charlie said. She has been talking to Zoë behind my back. I am unable to commit to anyone. Just like Zoë. My life is out of control. I hesitate in the entrance hall, wondering whether to go upstairs or down.

I decide to give Anthony a way out first and afterwards deal with Charlie. I run downstairs. Anthony is filling in time by unloading the dishwasher, piling all its contents on the bench as if he's preparing for a garage sale.

'She's home,' he says, his face expressionless. As if I didn't know.

'She's overwrought. I'm going upstairs to talk to her in a minute.'

'She's had a shock,' he says. But he does not mention his own.

'Yes.' There is so much to say that I feel there is nowhere to begin; the prospect of telling Anthony of what has happened fills me with dread, like the thought of beginning to cart away a mountain with a small hand trowel. Anyway I have to speak to Charlie first. I feel tired, drained. Anthony and I stand there in the kitchen like two strangers not knowing what to say to each other.

'I'll go home now,' he says at last.

And he leaves. He does not kiss me goodbye.

37

NOW

'Where's Anthony?' Charlie is sitting up in bed. The lamplight falls obliquely on her face so that it is half in shadow, and I see only an illuminated cheekbone, the line of her nose, and a bright and glittering eye that is staring at me intently.

'He's gone home.' I perch on her desk chair.

'What was he here for?'

'He flew over to see me, believe it or not.' I am having some trouble accepting it myself.

'Did you know he was coming?'

'No.'

'Are you seeing him again before he goes?'

'I don't know, Charlie.'

'He should've warned you he was coming.'

'What difference would that have made?'

'I would have been a bit more prepared.'

'It doesn't matter, Charlie.'

'Perhaps it's as well he's found out,' Charlie says.

She is right of course. Anthony had to know at some time too. She begins to tear the tissue she is holding into narrow ribbons. 'You led me to believe Dad was good and kind,' she continues, concentrating ferociously on what she is doing with her hands. 'Why all those lies?'

'I never told you he was good and kind.'

'You did by omission. It's what you didn't tell

222

me. By not explaining what he was like you created a misleading picture of him.' Charlie looks up at me. In her lap the methodically shredded tissue lies in tatters. 'And it's not just that he was violent. It's also about how he died. I saw what happened in the old newspapers, Mum. Not long after Dad got out on bail, there it was on the third page of *The Times*: ZOË'S ATTACKER FOUND DEAD. So I thought, ah well, that's when my dad had his massive heart attack, after all the stress. Then I read on. I was looking for details of his heart attack but there was nothing there. And why was that? Because he didn't die of a heart attack. The coroner said he had a subdural haematoma and then he choked to death. Those were the words the newspaper reported: *choked to death on his own vomit*.'

Sickened, I have to stop myself from bending my thumbnails back with my forefingers, a nervous reaction that I know irritates Charlie. Nausea and vomiting are symptoms of acute subdural haematoma, as are seizures and loss of consciousness.

'Mum, what a horrible end. Think of it.'

'Charlie,' I say at last. 'Don't think I've never thought of it.' After the coroner's report, I'd thought of little else. Jeff lying on a floor somewhere. Lying there, dying. The haematoma causing intense pressure on his brain. His mind sliding into unconsciousness, his last thoughts slipping away.

'But you couldn't bring yourself to tell me. And bloody Zoë couldn't either.'

Zoë, bloody Zoë. Jeff's way of death has been

223

our shared secret, our bond over the years.

'Everything always has to be perfect with you.' Charlie begins to roll the shreds of tissue together into a ball between her two palms. 'I never misbehave because I'm frightened you'll fall to bits. You never misbehave because you're frightened I'll fall to bits. It's all a bloody fabrication. I had a lousy dad! Why couldn't you tell me about it?'

'He wasn't all lousy. Nothing's ever black and white. He had some good points.'

'Oh come on, Mum, admit it! Did you love him so much that you couldn't see it? Or are you so frightened of making a mistake that you can't admit that you ever did?'

'No,' I tell her firmly. 'I've made lots of mistakes.' At this point I realise something; something so obvious I wonder how it could have taken so long. Although marrying Jeff was a mistake ex post, it was not a mistake ex ante. It wasn't my fault the marriage went sour; it was something that couldn't have been predicted beforehand. I wasn't to blame for his violence either; that was the way he was. I hadn't picked badly because I couldn't have known beforehand about this. So I didn't deserve to be punished for my choice.

Perhaps Helen has a point. I store this thought away to retrieve later and I look at my daughter's tired and pallid face.

'I think you couldn't handle me knowing what a flawed man Dad was because it reflected badly on you,' she is saying. 'Because it showed that you'd chosen badly.'

Her accusations line themselves up like

landmines between us; cross this gap at your peril. I want to reach out to her but am afraid of further damage. She has a right to be angry; I should have told her earlier. In her shock she is shifting to me the weight of her anger, her anger at losing the simple certainties of childhood.

'I'm so sorry about all this, Charlie,' I say at last. My apology sounds lame but I have to continue. 'I wanted to protect you. And I didn't want to tell you the circumstances of his death. It was all so sordid. It would have been a hard burden for you to bear as a little kid.'

'Would you have told me if I hadn't found out?'

'Yes. I was planning to.'

'You should've explained. It's like telling a child about being adopted. It's something I needed to know.'

'It's not like being adopted. There's no need for you to know everything that happened between your parents.'

'This wasn't everything.'

'But which is worse, Charlie — knowing how he died or knowing that I concealed this from you?' I look at Charlie's slender hands engaged in pulling apart her shredded ball of tissue. She doesn't reply; she is now tearing the strips of tissue into little squares of confetti.

'I fell asleep at Zoë's place,' she says abruptly. 'But I woke up suddenly with horrible images whirring through my head. At first I thought I was dreaming and then I realised what I'd thought was a dream was probably a memory dredged up from the past. Of you and Dad.'

225

'What was it about?'

'You were sitting at the dining room table in Islington. You had your contact lens container in front of you, and you were looking at your finger-tip.' Charlie mimes the actions: she examines her extended forefinger, which she is holding up some twenty centimetres in front of her face.

'Dad was standing next to you shouting,' she continues. 'You didn't seem to be taking any notice of what he said. Then you got down on your hands and knees to look at the carpet. Dad got down with you, and you both crawled all over the floor. Neither of you noticed me standing in the doorway. I think I was supposed to be upstairs asleep.

'Normally I would have thought that the sight of my parents crawling around the floor was comical. You looked like two farmyard animals grazing across a field. But I didn't laugh. I knew there was something wrong. You inched around the table on your hands and knees, all the way back to where you'd started from.'

' "It's vanished," you told my dad. ' "How strange." '

Charlie's face is intent. She is somewhere else, back in that memory, the one that I try to forget.

'You smiled at my dad. But he didn't smile back. He shouted at you again, very loudly. I can't remember what he said, but it was clear he was very angry.'

'I'd lost my contact lens, Charlie.'

'I remember seeing Dad patting his hands across the tabletop, feeling every part of its surface. After that you got down on all fours again and carried on looking. But while you were on the floor, Dad suddenly turned and kicked you very hard in the stomach. Twice.' Charlie pauses. She doesn't look at me. 'Is this true, Mum? Not just a faulty memory?'

'Yes, Charlie. That's what happened. More or less.' I am beginning to feel faint. I grasp my knees and lean forward. Memory is my enemy; I want to move forwards not back.

'After I saw Dad kick you, I turned tail and raced upstairs. I'd forgotten all about seeing this, Mum, until I woke up there on Zoë's sofa a few hours ago. And you know what I thought? That I was a coward because I didn't stay to defend you.'

'Don't cry, Charlie.' I get out of the chair and sit on the edge of her bed. I hold her in my arms while she sobs like a small child. 'Everything's going to be all right,' I say; although I'm not at all sure that it is.

'Memory's a funny thing,' Charlie continues when she's dried her eyes. 'I might have seen other things that I don't recall. On the way home in the taxi I thought I might have made up that incident about the contact lens. That I might have, like, invented it after reading about Dad and Zoë.'

'No, it was true.'

'Did he hit you often, Mum?'

'Often enough.'

'I hope I'm not violent.' Charlie's voice is casual, as if this thought has just occurred to her.

Taking her hand, I say, 'You're definitely not violent.'

227

'What if it's genetic?'

'Charlie, I don't believe that genes determine the way people act.' I put my arms around her again. 'Lots of non-genetic factors affect your behaviour. Genes might determine your susceptibility to certain influences, but they're not going to make you violent or non-violent.'

Charlie rests her head on my shoulder and I kiss her hair, soft and smooth and smelling faintly of shampoo.

'Your father wasn't genetically violent,' I continue. 'He was spoilt as a child because he was delicate, and he never learned to control his anti-social tendencies. Who knows, had he lived longer he might have learned eventually. That was his tragedy.'

We sit in silence for a few minutes. The old clock in the dining room chimes the quarter hour. It's four-fifteen and I suddenly feel drained, as if a plug has been pulled and my emotions have trickled away leaving behind a shell of a woman. But I can't stop now. I take a deep breath and say, 'There's something else that I need to tell you, Charlie.'

38

THEN

Barely a week after Jeff's assault of Zoë first hit the newspaper headlines, and a few days after Charlie and I escaped to Coverack, I returned to London again to collect some things I'd forgotten to pack in the rush to get away. There was a file of notes in particular that I needed in order to finish my thesis. Charlie stayed with my parents while I caught the train home; my visit was to last no more than two nights and Charlie seemed content to stay on at Coverack.

My first evening back was wet and depressing, and colder than it should have been in summer. I sat at the kitchen table in front of my laptop, and struggled to collect my thoughts about the chapter I was writing. When the intercom outside the house rang, I was tempted to let it go but thought better of it. Though the bell was working the voice connection wasn't — that was another thing to add to the list of repairs to give the landlord — and I ran down the stairs before the intercom could ring again. Mrs Gates from the ground floor flat had her television on relatively low but I could still hear every note of the theme music from *EastEnders*. I opened the door and was shocked to see Zoë standing there, dripping water onto the doormat. Conversation with Zoë wasn't something I wanted my neighbour to overhear. It wasn't that Mrs Gates was unfriendly, just nosy. Too nosy, she knew everything that was going on in our little street and more besides, and who knew what secrets Zoë might give away. She had no umbrella with her; her mackintosh was soaked through and water dripped from it into a puddle at her feet.

'You'd better come in.' I couldn't bear to look at Zoë's lovely face; it wasn't that I begrudged her that beauty but more that the black bruise and the swollen ocular orbit and that line of stitches above the eyebrow were reminders of what I'd rather forget.

Zoë followed me up the steep stairs to my flat. I took her dripping raincoat and hung it from the peg behind the front door. 'Come into the kitchen,' I said. 'I've got the gas fire on; it will dry you out a bit.'

I felt embarrassed for my ugly shabby flat, the walls baby-blue above the dado rail and the flock wallpaper below of a nasty green and orange paisley pattern that might have been here for decades, the carpet a speckled brown. But why should I mind what Zoë thought? Of course I realised right away that posing this question meant I did care, and rather too much, so I followed it up with an additional thought to myself: *who the bloody hell cares?*

'It's very light and bright,' Zoë said once we were in the kitchen. And it was. It was made so by the rice paper light fitting with the hundred-watt bulb, and the planet lamp on the table, as well as by the clean white walls that I'd painted the week after Charlie and I moved in.

I'd known right away that I couldn't live and work in a room that was painted lime green. The landlord had agreed that I could do this as long as I paid for the paint myself. It took a lot of coats to conceal that lime green.

Zoë added, 'You're working. I'm sorry to disturb you.'

'Would you like some tea?'

When she nodded, I turned away and busied myself with the kettle and tea things, a kind of therapy for the agitation I felt at her presence. It was as if the very air molecules — the nitrogen and oxygen, not to mention carbon dioxide and methane — were knocking hard together and creating a kind of turbulence in my kitchen.

She said, 'The police have put a non-molestation order on Jeff.'

Struggling to breathe, I stopped what I was doing.

Zoë continued, 'He's not allowed to see me. He's in a terrible rage. He called me not long ago, in spite of the order.'

'I see.' I began to feel queasy. 'Did you phone the police?'

'Not yet.'

'How did you know I was here?'

'I rang your parents. You gave me their landline number, remember? You wouldn't give me your mobile number.'

'I hope you didn't tell him I was back in London.'

'Of course not.

'So why are you here? I suppose you wanted to see where Charlie and I live.'

'That wasn't it at all,' she said, her tone dignified. 'I don't pry. I've come because I wished to return your scarf. You left it at my place the other day.'

'Did I? I wondered where it was.'

From her shoulder bag she retrieved a clear plastic bag containing the blue and green silk square that my mother had given me years ago and that I'd been upset to lose. When I took it from her, our hands touched. Hers were cold and wet. As I passed her the hand towel — it looked none-too-clean — I said, 'Thanks for bringing it back.'

She sat at the table. I pushed my laptop to one end and arranged my papers in a pile, each journal article arrayed like basket weave. Once she left I'd be easily able to restore the apparent disorder that I liked to work in, my materials and notes looking a total mess but placed so I could find them right away.

There seemed to be nothing more to say once the kettle had boiled, and I wished her gone. We sat in front of our mugs of tea and listened to the traffic go by and the drip-drip-drip of the kitchen tap whose washer needed replacing. It was almost a relief to hear a knock at my front door. It had to be my neighbour. You could only gain access to the flats by ringing the outside intercom and being let in. 'It will be Mrs Gates from downstairs,' I said at the same moment that Zoë said, 'I should go home.'

We both stood up. She followed me out of the kitchen. When I opened the door to my flat I was horrified to see Jeff on the landing. Even though he was standing a metre away I could detect the whisky on his breath, and his pupils were dilated. Swaying slightly, he said, his words running together, 'I know you've got her here.'

'Do you indeed? Well, you're wrong. Charlie's at Coverack.'

'I'm aware of that, you idiot. I'm looking for Zoë. I saw her arrive.'

'How did you get in?'

'You left the downstairs door ajar.'

I glanced down the stairwell. The front door was wide open and I could feel the cold draught blowing through. He hadn't even bothered to push it to. Rain was driving in onto the tiles.

'You should be more careful.' He laughed in a mirthless sort of way. 'But I'm glad you're not.'

It was the creaking of the floorboards behind me that gave Zoë's whereabouts away, for she wouldn't be visible from the landing outside the door to my flat. The door opened the wrong way: all that would be seen from the landing was the door to the bedroom and that was shut.

'Let me in.' Jeff's words were slurred and his tone angry.

I stood firm. He took a step closer, so close that I could see through the opening of his shirt the blond chest hair. It repulsed me. He raised his fist as if to strike me. It was fear or anger or both that made my heart begin to race like a wild creature in my throat, and adrenaline pump through my system, telling me to take flight. Yet there was nowhere for me to go. I couldn't let him into my flat. I wouldn't let him into my flat.

He expected me to take a step back but I

didn't. By this time I knew that Zoë was standing right behind me and that Jeff could now see her. I heard her sharp intake of breath as Jeff raised his hand. He smacked my face hard. Though I could feel my cheek stinging, I ignored the blow. Stepping forward, I shoved him on the chest with both hands. He lost his balance, and pirouetted on the landing in front of me for a second that seemed to stretch into infinity. I couldn't help noticing how graceful he was, even when drunk, even when trying to regain his balance. As graceful as a ballet dancer.

He appeared oblivious of the banister to his side, unmindful of the steep drop behind him, or perhaps he was just so drunk that he didn't know quite where he was. I got as far as raising my hand to reach out to still that endless pirouette. But I waited a fraction too long and I was too late to secure him. Abruptly, as if it had a will of its own, my hand dropped by my side. As in a slow motion movie, he fell backwards down the staircase. His body made a thumping sound on the stair treads as it fell. At the bottom lay that tessellated encaustic tile floor. He landed hard onto it and his body crumpled up. But it crumpled elegantly. Even in an accident Jeff was stylish. He didn't cry out. It was possible that nothing would break him. But he was very still.

For a moment neither Zoë nor I said anything, and my limbs felt as if paralysed. It was the eruption of Mrs Gates through her front door that broke the spell. 'I saw him hit you a minute ago,' she said. 'So I rang the police.'

'Better ring for the ambulance too.' Zoë pulled

234

her mobile out of her pocket.

'That mightn't be necessary,' Mrs Gates said.

Jeff was already sitting up. He looked shaken but I was relieved that he was able to get to his feet. Mrs Gates backed away yet she needn't have worried. Though Jeff was now standing upright, he was less steady on his feet than before his fall. He didn't look at any of us as he turned away and lurched out the front door. This time he slammed it shut so hard that its stained glass panels undulated slightly but they did not shatter.

By this point I was starting to worry about what the police would say when they learned that I had shoved him. Did I push him down the stairs or did I just push him away from Zoë and me? Whatever I'd done, it was in self-defence. But I was glad he could walk away.

'Did you see anything?' Zoë called out to Mrs Gates.

'Yes, like I said. I heard quite a ruckus with all that shouting and when I came into the hallway and looked up I saw him hit Sally. Who is he?'

'My husband,' I said, my voice cracking. 'We're separated though.'

'Can't say I blame you, love.'

'We'll tell the police exactly what happened,' Zoë said to me, her arm around my shoulders. 'He shouldn't have been trying to reach me, not with that non-molestation order, and he was about to beat you up. Well, he'd already begun, hadn't he? That was quite a blow to your face. You'll be bound to get a bruise. There's a big red mark there and his signet ring must have cut the skin, there's a bit of blood too.'

I pulled a tissue from my pocket and dabbed at the drops of blood. Already my cheekbone was starting to throb.

'And he would have begun on me next,' Zoë added. 'If you hadn't stopped him.'

'I know. You're the reason he was here,' I said.

'The only person to blame is Jeff,' Zoë said firmly. 'It's not you. It's not me. It's Jeff. You're brave, Sally. And don't you forget it.'

'The worm has turned,' I said.

Uncertain whether to laugh or cry, I sat down on the top step and noted dispassionately that I had begun to shake all over. I was still sitting there, shivering as if I had a fever, when the police arrived and Zoë, assisted occasionally by Mrs Gates, guided them through an account of what had happened. Later it was my turn. Later; after I'd recovered from the shock.

39

NOW

'And that was just the beginning of it,' I tell Charlie. Of course I've given her an edited version of what happened that dreadful night. I haven't mentioned that I got as far as raising my hand to reach out to still Jeff's seemingly endless pirouette. I haven't mentioned that I've sometimes wondered since then if I might have saved him from that fall.

Zoë and Mrs Gates were good witnesses and I'm sure it helped me that Jeff had ignored the non-molestation order the police had taken out on Zoë's behalf. It was clear to everyone that I had pushed him in self-defence. Lightly I touch my cheekbone. Jeff's blow to my face that night had broken the skin, and left a blotch that took months to fade. Zoë's face was marked forever by Jeff's assault. Though the cut above her eye had healed quickly, it left a thin scar that even now, even after all those years, bisects her left eyebrow.

'After he fell down the stairs that night,' I tell Charlie, 'we thought he was OK. He got up almost immediately and was out the front door as quick as can be, and at that stage no one knew where he went.'

I stand and pace around Charlie's bedroom as I struggle to find the words to describe what happened later. Omitting the ghastly details, I begin to relate an abridged version. The terrible anxiety I'd felt after learning after the inquest of the subdural haematoma that can come on after a major trauma to the head. Usually within twenty-four to forty-eight hours, but sometimes even longer. And the substances he'd been taking hadn't helped.

Once I'd identified him at the mortuary, things started to get serious. You'd think I might have thought about this on the train back to London to view his body but I hadn't. It had been a terrible shock to discover that I was to be extensively interviewed under caution by officers from the Criminal Investigation Department.

★ ★ ★

In the interview room, a solicitor was sitting next to me, a short woman with a deep voice that seemed surprising for her slim frame. How she got there I had no idea. The CID men sat opposite me. The older one had a head like a hard-boiled egg that could be cracked open with a spoon, and with pale blue, watery eyes that left my face only to glance at his notes. The second man was tall and stooping, with black hair going grey around the temples and a long narrow nose that looked as if it had been broken once or twice. Like burrs on a woollen sock, these details adhere to my memory.

The confusing emotions that meeting gener-ated are also with me still. Relief and guilt. Relief at knowing that the burden of what had happened to me over the years was at last known to the police and that it couldn't happen again now that Jeff was dead. Guilt — which I kept bottled up tightly inside me — because I felt that I was responsible for Jeff's death.

Yet the substance of our conversation that day has mostly vanished from my head; I retain only the impression that it was more interrogation than interview. I can recall that they asked a lot of questions but I can remember only two of them. Was it really true that Jeff had been violent to me before? And if that was the case, why hadn't I gone to the police earlier to lodge a complaint?

While struggling to respond, again and again I had thanked Mrs Gates for calling the police. Not aloud of course, it was merely a refrain that penetrated my thoughts all through that interminable interview, like a mantra that kept me going. *Thank you, Mrs Gates. Thank you so much, Mrs Gates. What a good neighbour you are, Mrs Gates.* Without the logging of the incident at the top of the staircase that evening just a few days before, without Zoë's and Mrs Gates' witness statements, things might have gone far worse.

★ ★ ★

'In the end there was a decision not to prosecute,' I tell Charlie. 'They decided the circumstances amounted to justifiable and proportionate self-defence. Afterwards I slept for eighteen hours solid. Somehow my name was kept out of the news-papers but Zoë's wasn't.' Jeff had lost his identity by then; the media knew him solely as Zoë's assailant. Then they lost interest when the next scandal came along.

'Was that why you were away from Coverack for so long?' Charlie says.

'Yes.'

'I thought you were working. That's what Gran said.'

We sit in silence apart from the distant hum of late Saturday night traffic down the A-road half a mile away. Through the crack in the curtains I can see the orange of the sodium street lamps that give London streets such a characteristic light at night. Eventually I say, 'We wanted to protect you, Charlie.'

But there is no response. Turning away from the orange glow, I see that Charlie has fallen asleep sitting up. Just like that: here one minute and gone the next. Gently I ease her down onto the pillows, pull the duvet over her, and switch off the lamp.

The house feels cold; the central heating must have turned itself off hours ago. Quickly I brush my teeth and climb into bed but find I can't sleep. Thoughts crowd into my head; the events of the last twelve hours play and replay themselves. Jeff is still influencing our lives even though he's been dead for ten years. Jeff has come back to haunt us, and Anthony has gone.

In bed I cannot get comfortable. I wind the duvet round me like a roll around a sausage, its softness wrapping me in a warm embrace. Anthony was glad to make his escape from this household. Should I have left him in the kitchen while I spoke to Charlie? Afterwards I could have gone downstairs and explained my past to him. But that opportunity has gone. He will never contact me again now he knows what things are like here; now he has seen Charlie at her worst, now he knows about my past. I try not to think of him, I try not to think of the abrupt way we said goodbye.

I turn over again and feel for my tissue. Poor Charlie. The fixed points of her life are fixed points no longer. Perhaps I've protected her too much. She should know that Jeff was a weak man. His physical violence was the action of someone who was fundamentally weak. Perhaps if he had lived longer he might have learned to control his rages, perhaps he might have learned that these were destructive of that most valuable of things — the delicate relationship between human beings. But then again he might never have acquired this understanding. He might have continued to blame other people for his actions, and to view the violence he meted out to the women he said he loved as a punishment necessary for their own good.

I switch on my bedside lamp and sit up. I try opening the novel that I keep on the bedside table to read each night, but I am so tired it's impossible to concentrate. After five minutes I turn out the light again, but as soon as my head touches the pillow thoughts of Jeff come crowding, thronging back.

I remember the countless arrangements I made in the months after the inquest in order to establish a new life for Charlie and me. But something important had gone, Jeff had gone; and he took with him many of my dreams. Before Jeff's death I knew that our marriage was over, but I also knew that he was still there; the father of my child was still there. After he died the past flooded back, every action that I took was associated in some way with my earlier life with him.

It was such a painful process packing up the house in Islington that we'd once owned jointly and that I now owned completely, mortgage and all. Zoë offered to help me. We had become goods friends by then but I didn't want to do it with her. I needed to do it alone. I was not merely packing up material things — deciding what to keep, what to give away, what to throw away — I was also trying to pack up memories. Those memories of Jeff's and my life together could not be as easily disposed of as our material possessions. Those memories are baggage I shall always carry with me.

It's no use trying to sleep; I might as well get up again. I put on my dressing gown and go downstairs. The Scrabble board is still on the coffee table; the game Anthony and I will never complete. I look at the words spread out on the board. There is the word 'luck' that I put down, and which Anthony extended to 'lucky' with his addition of 'yard'. Lucky, that's what I am; lucky that Charlie came home. This is the most important thing. This is what I will focus on.

I sweep all the tiles into a heap in the centre of the board and slide the lot into the cardboard box. After picking up the vase of red roses from the floor, I restore it to the centre of the coffee table. The blooms, tight buds when I put them in water last night, have begun to open. By some trick of light they glow as if illuminated from within; they appear almost incandescent. I touch them but they feel cold and slightly clammy. I bury my face in the fleshy petals. The roses have no scent; they are bred only for their appearance.

A symbol of love.

They will be dead by the middle of the week.

I go down to the kitchen. There on the bench top is all the crockery that Anthony unloaded from the dishwasher.

He has an orderly mind; the dishes and glasses are ranked by size. I pull open the cutlery drawer, expecting to see the knives and forks similarly aligned. It's almost a relief to see that Anthony chucked them in, higgledy-piggledy, any old how. I put on the kettle and, while the water heats, look out the window. The dark sky is sparsely dusted with a few stars and to the east there is a streak of paler blue. It will soon be light.

Charlie's father was only fourteen years older than she is now when he died. She has a tough time ahead of her, reinterpreting the past after the loss of many of the old certainties. I wish it had all been different for her. I wish it had been as she's believed it to be up until today. I concealed the truth to protect Charlie. And she thinks I did it because I was protecting myself. That I am so frightened of making a mistake that I cannot admit that I ever did.

What were Charlie's exact words? Yes, I can

243

remember them now. 'Everything always has to be perfect with you.'

But it was not just that. I struggle against my fatigue to retrieve the thought I filed away after she had made that statement. It was important; I know it was important but it eludes me. I think that it had something to do with *ex ante* and *ex post*, before and after, but I can remember nothing more than this.

While I drink my tea, the clock chimes half-five. Exhaustion engulfs me. I go upstairs to the bathroom and wash my face. A pallid face with swollen eyelids looks back at me from the mirror over the washbasin. It's not an attractive sight. I return to bed, insert sponge plugs into my ear canals, and fall at once into a deep and dreamless sleep.

40

NOW

'Coffee, Mum.' I open my eyes to see Charlie standing by my bed, a steaming mug in her hand. The mug with 99% *PERFECT* stencilled on its side. She is smiling at me, her face tranquil and unmarked by the tears and emotion of last night. 'It's midday,' she says.

'Seize the day,' I mumble as I pull out the sponge earplugs and struggle to sit up. '*Carpe diem.*'

She puts the mug on the bedside table and perches on the edge of the bed. The back of my head is thumping, my neck and shoulders are stiff, my nerves are stretched taut.

'Love you, Mum,' she says.

Her words undo me and I begin to bawl, great wracking sobs that make my sinuses tingle. She puts her arms around me. Between sobs, I gulp out the words, 'I love you too.'

'I know,' she says. 'I know, I know. I'm sorry I worried you last night.' She pats my back as if I am a small child. I blow my nose, a loud trumpeting. After I'm calmer, she says, 'The Blake bloke's called. Twice.'

My heart begins to hammer hard and my throat becomes constricted.

'It's a miracle you didn't hear the phone. Some people will sleep through anything. I told him you'd call him back. By the way, is it OK if I go over to Amrita's this afternoon? The Blake bloke wants to see you today. He said something about a walk on the Heath.'

It is a moment before I can trust myself to speak. 'I'll call . . . ' I manage to say before a fit of coughing stops me. 'I'll call him in a minute.'

'I like him. We had quite a long chat this morning. Not about last night or any of that stuff.'

'What about?'

'Tico and school and climate change and emissions trading schemes.'

'I see. Quite a wide-ranging discussion.'

'We didn't cover the European Union though,' she says, smiling. 'Not like those men on the boat yesterday.'

'Anything else?'

'No. You can tell him about the other stuff. And don't worry. Our conversation wasn't an interview. Or at least not on my part. Just a chat.'

★   ★   ★

It is late afternoon. Anthony and I are sitting side-by-side on a bench on Hampstead Heath. I have told him most of the events of the past, most of the details of my marriage. He has to know everything, or nearly everything. He has anyway heard much of it when he was cornered in the living room during Charlie's and my outburst. He sits next to me, letting me unburden myself, saying little apart from the occasional murmur of encouragement. Like Helen he lets me take my time. I stare at the grass while I talk, occasionally glancing up to see his eyes on me. I feel tense; unsure of what he is thinking, my nerves on edge.

When I have finished, we sit in silence. Although he is still watching me, there appears to be no judgement in his eyes, only concern. But this can't be all, he can't be this perfect, and for a moment I wonder if he is secretly pleased to hear about Jeff's character. I think back to our lunch over two weeks ago. That day I'd been surprised by his reaction to the knowledge that I am a widow, surprised by the subtle change in his response. Subsequently I'd wondered if Anthony might have believed I was still in love with my husband. Even though I didn't feel threatened by the death of his fiancée, it was possible that he might have felt threatened by my status especially if, until our lunch, he had thought I was divorced.

But I am too cynical. Anthony stands up and holds out his hands to me. Relaxing, I take them; I take what he is offering. He pulls me up from the bench and envelops me in his warmth. My face is buried in his jersey, his smell. This is where we were less than a day ago, when he first arrived here from Heathrow. A few hours ago. A few aeons ago.

For some time we stand holding each other. Blue drains from the sky as evening draws in. A few people stroll past heading to the car parks nearby. Eventually he breaks the silence. 'What did Charlie mean by the toy boys?' he says.

I stiffen; I have been deceived, he is not

offering unconditional acceptance. 'Just a few affairs I had.' My voice is muffled, my face still in the fabric of his jersey. 'Flings or whatever.'

Although he is stroking my hair gently, he persists in his line of interrogation. ' "Use them then lose them," she said.'

'She was trying to be nasty.'

'I know. And she succeeded.' He lifts my chin with his hand. I look into his eyes; I am close enough to see the white specks in the blue iris, and the darker blue around the edge. 'Are you going to do that to me?' he says. 'Dump me when things start to look serious?'

Suddenly I feel angry, angrier than I have felt for years apart from in my recent sessions with Helen. I wriggle out of his embrace and back away from him.

'I can't listen to this,' I tell him. 'It's none of your business. You can just bugger off.'

'Sally, what's the matter?'

'It's the last straw! Who cares about a few men I slept with? They weren't serious and that was reciprocal. Why did you have to mention them? You've spoilt everything!'

'I thought we were getting the past into the open.'

'You're prying. It's immaterial. They were casual flings. I don't question you about your past relationships and I never will. Never would have.'

'I'm sorry I've upset you Sally. But surely you can see that this might matter? The past determines the future after all. Initial conditions matter.' He sounds as if he is giving a lecture to the first year undergraduates; his voice is calm and measured.

'What difference would it make to you?'

'Because I might understand if you're approaching me in the same fashion. To be used to prop up your ego. And for our relationship not to be developed any further beyond that prop. Sally, I want stability. I'm not sure if you do.'

I feel as if he has hit me. I know he has a point, and because he has a point I become even more enraged, like a spoilt child unable to handle any criticism. 'So if I tell you about the men I've slept with,' I shout, 'you can conclude I'm unwilling to commit. And then we can call the whole thing off, is that what you're saying? Save you wasting any more time on me, is that it, Anthony?' An elderly couple passing by arm-in-arm look at me in astonishment, no, it is with disapproval.

'All I'm saying is that if you do think about me as someone you might just have a casual fling with, I want to know. We should talk about it. I know you had a ghastly time in your marriage. How can it not affect you subsequently? Why should you trust men again?'

'So I'm damaged. Damaged goods.'

'No, Sally, love.' I hear his endearment, and discount it. I throw it away: it's meaningless, it's not for me.

'I shouldn't have brought this up right now,' he continues, still in his same calm tone. 'We do need to talk about it, but this is clearly the wrong time. I'm sorry; I've been an insensitive bastard.'

'Too late!' I cry. 'Too late!' I want him to

become angry so I can walk away. I wait for his reaction, I wait for his fury.

But he does nothing, and we stand staring at each other, like two boxers in a ring waiting for the right opportunity to make a feint.

Finally he says: 'I'm not going to hit you, Sally. I'm never going to hit you. And I'm not going away either.'

'More fool you!' I cannot really believe that I am behaving in this infantile fashion, but I continue on my chosen course of destruction. 'I'm off. You can make your own way home!' I march away. I shall leave Anthony behind; I shall walk out of his life.

'I'm not going anywhere,' he calls out, loudly but apparently calmly.

I don't look back but accelerate towards the woods. I have to get some distance between us.

41

NOW

It's almost dark, and it's cold and damp. Circling through the woods, I scuff up the mouldering leaves with my shoes. I've behaved badly and I've chosen this route of destruction. I could have ignored Anthony's question, I could even have responded with a joke, or I could simply have answered truthfully. But I chose to be provoked.

Anthony picked the wrong time to ask his question. I don't really know if his motives were noble as he claimed, or if they were based on simple prurience. Or jealousy.

Yet I could have learned this if I had allowed our relationship to develop. I could have waited to see, I could have given him the benefit of the doubt. Regret begins to drive away my annoyance. I stop walking in order to think more clearly.

Anthony travelled thousands of miles to see me. He hasn't raised his voice once to me; he has acted impeccably to me. And how have I responded? Badly. Badly, badly. I have discounted his past too, his loss of Katherine to cancer. His experience has been of bereavement. Like mine, but not like mine; his relationship had been developing but mine was already dead. He had something to look forward to, and something that was abruptly taken away. He has seen the suffering of someone he loved; he has lost someone he loved. He said that he was insensitive but I have been insensitive too. No one reaches forty without being affected by what has happened to them. Initial conditions matter, all scientists know that. But the environment matters too and the random events that impinge upon you and alter your destiny.

I should apologise to Anthony.

A rustling in the bushes nearby startles me. Darkness is descending fast and I haven't seen a soul for some time. Again I hear that sound, more a scratching than a rustling, and from higher up. Then I see the grey squirrel, transfixed on a branch of an oak tree. For a couple of heartbeats we size up each other before it scampers on.

Suddenly I understand. Transferral, this is what I've been doing, and I don't need Helen to explain it to me. I've shifted my anger with Jeff to Anthony. Like an immature adolescent, I've dumped it on him.

Suddenly I want to see him; I want desperately to see him. He wasn't going anywhere, he said, but that was half an hour ago. He will be on his way home by now. On his way home to his flat in Notting Hill, on his way home to pack his bag for the return to Massachusetts tomorrow. He will be writing off today's experiences, and preparing to move on.

I must see him again. Before it's too late.

I break into a jog, my rubber-soled shoes quiet on the bitumen paving. I sprint through rain so light it is like a mist, cold and cocooning. It blocks out all sound but my panting as I fight for breath. The woods are silent: not a human being, not a dog, not a bird around. And where is the bench Anthony and I were sitting on earlier? Nowhere in sight. In the fading light the trees all look the same, gnarled giants that must be hundreds of years old, and I wonder if I'm running in circles rather than retracing my steps. Water begins to trickle down my neck and I fear I'll never see Anthony again. I stop running and double over, a cramp clutching at my stomach. My heart is pumping too hard as I struggle to get air into my lungs.

The cramp goes, and I walk on more slowly, hoping I'm heading in the right direction. The trees open up. Now there is a grassy expanse beside the path and I almost trip over a bench. It could be the one we were sitting on earlier but there is no sign of Anthony. The mist presses down on me, heavy like my heart. I am too late: I have been an idiot. Exhausted, I collapse onto the wet timber seat.

At this moment I see a figure twenty metres away, standing on the grass, his back towards me. I call out Anthony's name and he turns. He has stayed here as he said he would; he has waited for me.

'I knew you'd come back,' he says, 'but I didn't expect you to take this long.'

Though I smile at him, he doesn't smile back. His hair is ruffled; his face expressionless. He looks older than his years and tired, almost vulnerable.

'I'm so sorry, Anthony,' I say.

I hold out both hands to him, the same

gesture that he used to me earlier. He reaches out and pulls me close. I rest my cheek against his, feeling his stubble against my skin. We hold each other tightly and do not speak. While we are standing there the mist lifts and soon I begin to hear the distant murmur of traffic from the road ringing the heath.

'Let's go back to my flat,' he says eventually.

And so we head back to South End Green car park. We do not touch each other again; we walk side-by-side like an old married couple after a quarrel.

42

NOW

I wake with a start. It's cold; the duvet has slipped off me and I'm naked. I fumble for it, then realise it's not mine; of a different fabric, it's slippery and cold to the touch. There's a glimmer of light from the open door and I'm not in my own bed. At this point I remember: I'm in Anthony's. Smiling, I reach out for him, but he is no longer beside me. The scent of him lingers though: Pears' soap and clean skin.

There is a lamp on the table next to the bed. I switch it on, a circle of bright light in this plain dark room. A peacock blue dressing gown is hanging from a hook behind the door. I get up and shrug it on; it's of soft wool, cashmere mix perhaps, not a fabric I would have predicted as Anthony's choice. Perhaps it was given to him by his parents. Or a former girlfriend. But that doesn't matter. I am the one wearing it now.

I walk across the carpeted hallway and stand at the doorway to the living room. Anthony is dressed; he is sitting at the large desk occupying one end of the room. There is a pile of papers in front of him; I watch him as he reads, so deeply absorbed that he hasn't heard me. His head is tilted at an angle, and his profile is silhouetted against the light from the desk lamp. He looks peaceful, he looks unshakeable.

I shift my weight from one foot to the other, and the floorboards under me creak in protest. Anthony raises his head. He smiles, he stands. I stay in the doorway as still as can be, unwilling to change anything, unwilling to spoil anything. He walks towards me; I watch his face, strong and reliable. He puts his hands on my shoulders and gently tilts me towards him as if I am a cardboard cut-out doll, so that my head is resting against his chest.

After a few moments he takes my hand and leads me into the bedroom. He slips the peacock blue dressing gown off my shoulders; he pulls off his jumper and trousers and throws them onto a chair. We lie next to each other on the cool sheets and pull the duvet over us. I feel his warm skin, his skin like silk; his back so smooth. And everywhere his hands, everywhere his gentle fingers, stroking, exploring, arousing. His soft mouth consumes me, and the room turns as we are caught up in spinning whorls of light, then a flash, a blinding flash, a shuddering of our bodies, our body.

This is what I should have been looking for. A man like Anthony.

And I've found him now.

Somewhere in his flat that I haven't yet properly explored, a clock chimes. An antique clock like mine, it counts out the hours; it's seven o'clock.

'I'll have to phone Charlie,' I say when the clock falls silent. 'And next I'll go home.'

43

NOW

It's Tuesday morning in late October. The gloomy grey sky pushes down so heavily it's a relief to be buzzed into the shelter of Helen's entrance hall. As I burst through the door, barely one minute late, I see her waiting for me at the top of the stairs, her face quizzical. I run up the stairs, giving a brief and breathless account of the traffic I've encountered, which she acknowledges with the smallest tilt of her head.

Once in her consulting room, I kick off my shoes and stretch out on the sofa. Today I have no trouble deciding on what to tell her. I talk about Anthony's surprise visit, about Charlie going AWOL, about Charlie discovering that her father died of a clot on the brain rather than a heart attack, and how she found out about her father's violence to Zoë and to me.

'Charlie was very angry with me at first,' I explain. 'She blamed me for not telling her earlier. She said I couldn't bear to admit the past was less than perfect.'

Helen says nothing. I wriggle my toes a little and wait. Surely she will write this down on her notepad. But there is no sound from behind me so I continue: 'She said she'd always known Jeff wasn't much of a father, but I shouldn't have concealed his violence and the manner of his death. I think she's right, Helen. I delayed telling her because I couldn't accept it. I needed to preserve the fiction that the past hadn't been so bad.'

'So you saw the failure of your marriage as your fault not Jeff's,' Helen says flatly.

'Maybe I did feel that his death was my fault. That if I hadn't left him he'd still be alive today.'

'So you viewed Jeff's violence as your fault and not as his?'

'No, Helen.' Persistence is her middle name. 'It's as I explained before — I never regarded his violence as my fault. His death maybe; in part.' I hesitate, thinking of the hard shove I'd given him that last evening, when he had punched me at the top of the stairs. Thinking of the way he'd pirouetted in front of me before bumping down the steep staircase onto that ghastly tiled surface below. Of how lucky I'd been that there were two witnesses to his act of violence, Zoë and Mrs Gates.

'But I've never regarded his violence as my fault.' I pause again, knowing that I have to get something clear in my head. I think of what Charlie said last Sunday morning, that everything always has to be perfect with me. And now I can remember the thought I filed away immediately after she had made that statement. Helen might have a point: maybe I did unconsciously think I deserved Jeff's punishment. But the reason for this is almost too subtle to articulate; no wonder I had trouble recalling it.

'You were talking about Jeff,' Helen reminds me.

'Yes. Talking and thinking about Jeff.' I've almost forgotten Helen, so preoccupied am I with my thoughts. 'I've realised something, Helen. Maybe you were right. When you're deciding to hook up with someone, you think about the probability of success or failure and you calculate the expected outcome.'

My words sound pompous; but that's what I am, a pompous academic. I shut my eyes and struggle on. 'Then, if you've had a good throw of the dice and the relationship works, you stay. You've done better than expected. If you've had a bad throw, you've done worse than expected. And what do you do when you discover that? It depends on how bad. But whatever the throw of the dice, there was never anything wrong with your initial decision. When you made your choice, you just did the best you could with the information you had at the time. And so you shouldn't think you were a failure.'

Helen says nothing and I am in no hurry to continue. I open my eyes again and observe that she has, since my last session, introduced an additional element into her peaceful stable room, a room in which all that has changed until now is her outfit and the flowers in her vase: a new painting is hanging on the wall at right angles to me. It's a watercolour of a semi-abstract landscape, perhaps somewhere in East Anglia; its strong horizontal lines define a vast sky. I wonder if Helen realises this change might have a profoundly unsettling effect on her patients. Not on me though; I am calm, I am tranquil.

I think of Anthony and the last Scrabble game

that we played, and the word 'lucky' that we had constructed on the board. There is so much luck involved when you choose a mate. Luck and the unconscious needs of your genetic makeup. Attraction has to do with genetics. You're attracted to someone because their genes are dissimilar to your own and by choosing that person you thereby ensure the best chance for survival of your genes. But as well as all this there is an element of luck, that simple twist of fate. The fact that my marriage to Jeff turned out to be bad didn't mean my judgement was flawed. And so I didn't deserve the punishment my husband had meted out.

'You were right, Helen,' I tell her. 'At some level I did think I deserved Jeff's violence. It was almost as if he was punishing me for my lack of judgement in picking him.' I pause and listen to Helen writing on her pad. I owe her an apology. 'And I was so aggressive to you when you said I felt I'd deserved it. I really must apologise for that.'

'That does not matter, Sally. But you misinterpret what I said to you. I did not ever say that you thought you deserved it. I merely asked you to consider the possibility that you might have felt that you deserved it.'

I laugh and struggle to sit up from my prone position on the sofa. I look around at Helen. She is regarding me benevolently, as if I am a child who has performed better than anticipated. 'You speak like a lawyer,' I say, 'dealing in niceties.'

'I speak like a psychotherapist,' she says, putting down her pen and pad.

I don't lie down again but sit cross-legged on Helen's sofa.

'You have made your own way to this conclusion,' Helen says. 'It has not always been easy.'

'Too right it hasn't. Can I ask you something personal?'

'No, Sally.'

'But I'm going to anyway. You can choose to ignore it. That's what life is, a series of choices.' Helen's calm expression doesn't alter, so I put my question to her, the one that has been on my mind for some time. 'Have you ever been in a violent relationship, Helen?'

'Yes, I have,' she says, with some hesitation. 'Many years ago. But that is all I am going to say to you about it. Ever.'

We look at each other. She smiles suddenly, her astonishingly sweet smile. I feel a great affection for her and yet I know next to nothing about her. We have a professional relationship not a personal one. And that is why I can now divulge something else about Jeff. Because our relationship is professional Helen will never tell anyone else. This is something that I won't reveal to Charlie, never to Charlie. She does not need to know this. But if I tell Helen maybe I can put it all behind me. I look at my watch; twenty-five minutes until the session ends.

'There's something else, Helen. It's confidential.' I lie down on the sofa again. I cross one leg over the other, noting as I do so that a small hole is developing in the toe of my tights.

Helen doesn't say anything right away. I wait,

listening to her silence and the blood thumping in my ears.

'What you tell me in this room is always confidential, Sally.'

I begin to talk. I tell her that since that terrible evening of Jeff's fall I've sometimes wondered if I could have brought about a different outcome, that if I'd acted quickly enough I might have been able to stop him tumbling down the stairs. My words, compressed for years, escape like gas out of an uncorked flask and for a few seconds I imagine them floating in the air above the sofa, before dissipating slowly. Afterwards, a feeling of acceptance, almost of peace, descends on me like a comforting blanket. I examine a yellow trapezium of sunlight that has appeared on the wall. Unnoticed by me while I have been talking, the morning has cleared. A chapter of my life is now closing.

I begin to feel detached, as if I am elevating to the ceiling. I look down to see Helen seated in her armchair, and there is my body, my carapace, lying supine on her sofa. I hover high above, floating and free.

'That's all we've got time for today, Sally.' Helen breaks the spell. 'Perhaps next time you will tell me how you and Jeff met. It might help you.'

'How?'

'Relating the beginning sometimes helps with coming to terms with the ending.' She gets to her feet, and glides across the room, halting before she reaches the door. Her eyes on her new painting, she says, 'Remember what you told me at the start of our session today. You said that when you chose Jeff you did the best you could with the information you had available at the time. You gained more information only subsequently. You couldn't have known he'd be violent back before you married, and so you shouldn't think you were a failure.'

These are the most sentences she's ever spoken continuously to me. When she's finished, like the perfect hostess she is she opens the door for me; she guides me out of her room.

'Thank you, Helen,' I say as I slip past.

'It has been a pleasure,' she says in her formal way. And then she shuts the door quietly behind me.

44

THEN

The night I met Jeff, I was wearing a dark brown dress and carrying an embroidered purse with tiny mirrors sewn onto it. The first words Jeff ever spoke to me, before we even exchanged names, were: 'Your dress is the same colour as your eyes.' He stared intently at me, as if his words had more meaning than a simple observation. My friend Mary and I had just arrived at the party, and Jeff was the first person I noticed. I was struck by his height and elegance, and the thick fair hair that was so beautifully styled it might have been sculpted out of marble.

Embarrassed by his scrutiny, I looked down at my dress. This was the first time I had worn it. It was made of crushed velvet, with a low neckline and cut on the bias. Its hemline was rather uneven; my mother had shortened it for me only a few days before I left home to start university. I touched the fabric lightly before glancing at Jeff again. He was still staring at me. I tried to stop the blush that began in my neck and moved inexorably up to my face. My cheeks hot, I smiled at him before looking around for Mary, but she'd vanished.

'You're good when you're smiling,' he said, as if our acquaintance had been longer than sixty seconds in somebody's shabby digs in a semi-detached house in Willesden Green.

'Paying compliments is a very old-fashioned method of seduction,' I said, continuing to smile.

'Would you prefer me to lunge at you instead?' he said, laughing. 'Anyway, you're much too young for me. Beautiful but young.'

'I've just turned eighteen.' Immediately I regretted telling him this. I should have said nearly nineteen. 'And anyway, you're much too old for me.'

'I'm twenty-three. Suave and sophisticated although, alas, still a student.'

'Not my type though,' I said, although I didn't mean it. He looked exactly my type.

'Being rude is the modern form of seduction. Everyone's doing rudeness now. In fact, rudeness is the new compliment. I read it in *The Observer* last Sunday.'

'Self-defence in my case, not rudeness,' I said, laughing.

'So you need protection from me?'

'No. I can look after myself.'

'Well, do let me get you a drink, or would that be an act of aggression?' He waited for an answer, as if his question was more than rhetorical.

'No, that would be wonderful. Red wine please.'

'Don't go away,' he said. 'I like you.'

I had no intention of going away. I knew no one at the party apart from Mary and her brother, a final-year urban design student at the Bartlett School, who had invited us. And now this handsome stranger. Clutching my mirrored purse as if it were a talisman, I watched him manoeuvre his way through the crowd. He moved gracefully, like an athlete or a dancer. I saw him talk briefly to Mary, who was standing with her brother next to the drinks table. Soon he began to weave his way back. I looked away: I didn't want him to see me observing him. I didn't want to seem too interested.

'You're Sally,' he said as he handed me a tumbler of red wine. 'And I'm Jeff Hector, the well-known clairvoyant. I knew as soon as I clapped eyes on you that you were a Sally. A laughing Sally.'

'A laughing jackass,' I said. 'You asked Mary my name just now. I might be a fresher but I'm not completely naïve.'

'Delighted to hear it,' he said, grinning. 'That augurs well for Day One of our relationship.'

'Night One,' I said, and blushed when I realised too late how this might be interpreted.

Someone put on some music. It was an old and rather scratchy recording of The Eagles, *One of These Nights*. Jeff asked me to dance. In spite of the crowded room, he did not touch me. We danced as if there were an invisible barrier between us preventing us from moving closer, almost as if there were a physical force holding us apart.

But once the dancing had ended, we moved together and held each other. His hands and arms felt strong and comforting and we stayed like that for a long time. Then I pulled back to look at him. His eyes were glowing, his expression teasing, as he said, 'I'll let you go, just this once.'

45

NOW

A few days after I told Helen about first meeting Jeff, a few days after she gave me a month's notice, I dreamed of identifying his body as it lay on the gurney in that cold, cold mortuary. When I awoke, my pulses were racing and the stink of disinfectant mingled with ammonia was so strong in my nostrils that I could almost taste it. Some time later I fell asleep again, and dreamed of his warm body next to mine on our trip to La Spezia all those years ago. I drifted in and out of consciousness, and dreamed of him lying asleep next to little Charlie, a storybook open on the bed next to them. I awoke with a jerk, my pillow damp and an acid taste in my mouth. It took me a while to realise all that was more than ten years ago.

Now it is Friday evening. Charlie is out seeing a film with Amrita, and Zoë and I are alone in my living room. Zoë has been working in Amsterdam and it's been weeks since I last saw her. She is lying stretched out on the sofa, and on the coffee table between us is the bottle of Sancerre that she brought with her. It is standing sentinel next to a plate of vegetables cut into strips and a couple of bowls of dips that I picked up on the way home from work.

'How are things going with Helen?' Zoë asks.

'I told her about Jeff's accident. I hadn't been going to but I did.'

'And what did she say?'

'Nothing.'

'Surely she said something, darling.' Zoë sits up so abruptly that she sloshes a few drops of wine onto her blouse. This she ignores as she raises her eyebrows almost to her hairline. The scar that bisects her left eyebrow puckers a little. With her raised eyebrows, bright red lipstick, and heavily made-up face she looks like a caricature of a clown expressing astonishment.

'Helen never says anything much. Sometimes she makes probing little comments if things are going slowly but that's about it.'

'Comments like what?'

'Like when she asked if I thought it was my fault Jeff hit me.'

'She asked you that?' Zoë raises her eyebrows again.

'Yes.'

'So if I saw her, she might ask if I thought it was my fault Jeff punched me because I scraped his bloody precious BMW.' She takes a sip of wine as if it is medicine.

'She was surprised I stayed with him.' I walk to the window facing the back yard. Placing a hand on the pane of glass, I feel its coolness. A crisp half-moon illuminates the garden and casts deep shadows on the tiny lawn.

'It's not like Jeff's life was insured,' Zoë says. 'Nothing material hinged on whether it was an accident or manslaughter.'

This is what it reduces to, I think as I watch

the shadows flicker across the lawn and the last few autumn leaves drift to the ground. Nothing material hinged on the circumstances around Jeff's death. 'Helen has given me notice,' I tell Zoë.

'What, like an employee?'

'Yes. She said I don't need her any more. One month's notice — that's the deal.' My life for months has been measured out in Tuesday mornings.

'Good. What will you talk about for the next month then?'

'Stream of consciousness stuff, I expect. I'll see what comes up.'

'Life's too short to be endlessly contemplating your navel,' Zoë observes.

'Especially at eight o'clock in the morning.'

'Did you tell Anthony about Jeff's fall?'

'Not the details. Too complicated. I told him everything except that though.'

'You know, darling, Anthony's probably glad you didn't have a perfect bloody marriage. It means he won't be competing with some ideal. He might actually prefer you human rather than perfect.'

'Maybe.' I keep my voice non-committal. *A perfect bloody marriage.* It was far from that. But I doubt if I'll tell Anthony any more about it. At the moment I'm taking things with him a day at a time, and the days are good. Very good.

'I wonder if Charlie's been damaged by all this, Zoë. Knowing the way her father died. Knowing he was violent.' I don't need to add what lies unstated between us — that Charlie has learned that Zoë was her father's lover. 'Quite a shock.'

'That's an understatement, Sal. But she never idealised Jeff, so I think she'll be OK. The odd thing is, she doesn't blame me either. I thought she might . . . she might think I'd caused his death by taking him away from you.'

'You've spoken about all this?'

'On the phone last week. I called her up when I came home for a flying visit. She'd left a note in my flat for me.'

I suppose there's a lot that Zoë and Charlie talk about that they never tell me. This thought makes me feel slightly left out. Suddenly I think of Charlie's accusations about my boyfriends. I'd intended to raise this with Zoë at some stage, but now is not the time. Perhaps I never shall; perhaps it's time that I stop trying to protect Charlie from the past.

Zoë adds, 'Charlie left her note right next to the half-empty bottle of cognac. I'm glad she's normal.' She grins and I grin back. In a moment we are laughing, leaning over and clutching ourselves while we gasp for breath. Gusts of hilarity, convulsing paroxysms of mirth; I laugh while my stomach aches, we laugh until tears run down our faces.

When we have recovered I ask Zoë a question that has occurred to me a few times over the years. 'Have you ever felt guilty about breaking up my marriage to Jeff?'

'No. I did you a service.'

'You're amoral. I've always known that.'

'So have I. It's one of my many virtues.'

'I've felt guilt, Zoë. Quite a lot over the years. Relief mainly, but guilt as well. I could have pushed Jeff less hard.'

'For God's sake, Sally, how could you possibly gauge exactly how hard to push the bastard? How could you possibly anticipate the haematoma? He'd punched you once already that evening and really hard too. He would have hit you again, you can bet on that. He was as angry as hell. It was you or him, don't you see? It could have been you tumbling down the stairs, you landing on your head, you with a fractured spine or worse. And who would have looked after Charlie then? Not him, he couldn't be trusted. You did right and you mustn't ever think otherwise. I thought you'd got all of that out of your system years ago. And the bits you hadn't got out of your system by now I thought the shrink was supposed to be extracting.'

'Maybe I should tell Charlie that I might have been able to stop Jeff's fall.'

'For heaven's sake, Sally. You're the only person who's ever thought that you could have done that. I was standing right next to you. There wasn't a cat in hell's chance you could have stopped him tumbling down those stairs. Charlie already knows that. It's one of the things we spoke about.'

'Did you? She didn't tell me.'

'She's a sensitive young woman. And she felt bad that she'd worried you that night she was so late home. You couldn't ask for a better daughter than Charlie. Full credit to you my friend.'

I swill down half my glass of wine and almost

at once my body feels lighter, as if it might float away. My vision sharpens and I begin to see the room as if for the first time. Everything has meaning: Zoë's face, as lovely as ever; the pieces of red and green pepper and sliced carrots on the plate; the pool of light reflecting on the polished timber floor; the framed photographs on the bookshelves.

'Jeff wasn't to know we'd become friends,' Zoë says. 'But we got the last laugh.'

'He certainly can't take that away from us.'

'He can't take anything away from us.' She picks up the crudités platter and offers it to me. While crunching up a carrot stick, she says, 'By the way, you do know that Charlie wants to visit Jeff's grave, don't you? What will you do?'

'Take her of course.' I glance at the Sancerre. There's half a bottle left to drink in front of the movie we're planning to download. 'But I really don't want to go.'

'But you will, Sally.' Zoë laughs, while leaning forward to touch my hand lightly. 'You're always the model mum,' she says.

46

NOW

A dense layer of clouds, relentlessly sombre, presses down on London. Today is 29 November. It is exactly eighteen years since I married Charlie's father.

We join the M4 motorway and are caught up in a stream of traffic that is going too fast. Charlie, in charge of the music, plays compromise CDs that neither of us much likes. Beyond Reading, the clouds roll away and the landscape opens into the rolling green fields of Wiltshire, austerely beautiful. The trees, denuded of all leaves, reveal their structure: strongly buttressed trunks that taper to delicate lacework silhouetted against the pale sky.

The M4 gives way to the M5 and we exit in the Somerset Levels. At a supermarket we stop to buy flowers. I wait in the car while Charlie chooses them, a cellophane-wrapped bunch of white lilies. It is mid-afternoon by the time we reach the churchyard at Burnham-on-Sea. Charlie needs time alone at her father's grave, she has said. After I find a parking place, she opens the passenger door. In her hand she holds the map I drew before leaving Kentish Town, the map of the churchyard that will show her where Jeff is buried. Her clenched jaw betrays her anxiety as she says, her words barely audible,

'Can you meet me back here in one hour?'

I check my watch and she shuts the car door, too hard as usual. She strides along the gravel path leading to the far side of the churchyard, as if she is late for an appointment. My mobile phone pings, a text message from Anthony wanting to know if we've arrived safely. I tap out a reply promising to phone him later.

To fill in time I walk to the seafront. Opposite the promenade, a long row of Georgian and Victorian houses gaze vacantly seaward, over the concrete sea wall and the mud flats. The tide is out, and the expanse of mud stretches for perhaps half a mile towards the sea that is barely visible in the hazy late afternoon light; the palest blue-grey sky bleeding into grey-brown water.

When I first visited this town with Jeff, so many years ago, I hated the decaying splendour of its old houses and the modern additions made to hold the structures together. The double glazing, the stucco, the awnings providing shelter against the harsh weather, the pinball parlours. Even the once elegant old pier building was clad in the least attractive and cheapest materials that modern technology had to offer. But now I see the town in a new light. I admire its determination to fight the elements; to provide a Mediterranean-inspired seaside resort from the most unpromising raw materials; to pretend that here there is a beach and not an expanse of flat colourless mud.

The last time I was here was for Jeff's funeral. Zoë and I arrived together. She caught the train down from London and I came up from

Coverack; we'd arranged to meet up at the nearest station and share a minicab from there. Zoë, dressed in black as usual, and with the fading yellow bruise around her eye that she hadn't concealed with make-up, was an embarrassment to Jeff's family. No one could avoid looking at her injury but no one was going to comment on it. The mark on my cheekbone went unnoticed, covered with concealer I'd bought in Falmouth. Jeff's father appeared old and grey and tired. He watched the proceedings gimlet-eyed, shattered by the loss of his son but unable to express his feelings. We shook hands after it was all over, but he didn't look me in the eye. Afterwards Zoë and I caught a taxi to the station: she was in a hurry to get back to London, and I to Cornwall.

As I walk along the esplanade, a grey mist begins to roll in from the sea. The town becomes almost beautiful when there is no sun, in winter like this, when the harsh colours of the houses come into their own. The softening mist blurring things, like the passage of time.

By the time I return to the church, the light has almost gone. I cannot see Charlie anywhere. I walk straight to Jeff's grave, on the far side of the graveyard. I look at the gilded curlicued lettering inscribed on the polished black granite headstone: 'Jeff Hector, The Ideal Son,' and underneath the dates of his birth and death. *The Ideal Son.* I had never understood this choice of words. Yet perhaps to Jeff's parents he had been the ideal son: handsome, clever, creative. Jeff wouldn't have liked the headstone his father chose. It could certainly not be described as minimalist. The black granite embellished at the top with an intricately carved branch of gilded roses.

I run my fingers over the roses. Jeff's birth date is almost two years earlier than Anthony's. Strangely I have thought of Jeff as always young, as so much younger than Anthony. Poor Jeff, my pitiful weak husband. He missed out on so much. Saddest of all, he missed out on seeing his daughter grow up.

So much has happened since Jeff died, and yet nothing has happened. The world spins on while places stay still in our minds. Still and fixed, while we are swirling around them, whirling through time, revolving through space.

Below Jeff's headstone is Charlie's bunch of lilies arranged in a large jar of water. The lilies give out a strong scent of midsummer that seems incongruous in the wintry setting. Charlie herself is still nowhere to be seen.

Perhaps she has gone into the church and I try to open its weathered oak door. It is firmly locked. Eventually I find her sitting on a bench in the older section of the graveyard. Dressed in black, she is almost invisible against the dark backdrop of a yew tree. Only her pale hair and paler face indicate her whereabouts.

'Hiya, Mum,' she says when she sees me. 'Bit early, aren't you?'

I look at my watch. 'Spot on time.'

'Sit down for a minute,' she says. 'It's nice here. Like, peaceful.'

I sit down on the bench next to her. The wood

feels damp. 'Are you all right?' I ask.

'Yes. I'm glad we came. Did you see my flowers?'

'Yes, they look lovely.'

'Funny idea really. To stick flowers on a grave, as if the dead person could see them.'

'Well it's not for them. It's for the living.'

'I know.' She smiles: I see the gleam of her teeth in the fading light. 'They're for me. And I feel better for it.'

We sit in silence for a few more minutes. Then she says: 'Are you OK, Mum?'

This is the first time she's ever asked me this. I feel touched to the centre of my being; I don't trust myself to reply.

'You're crying, Mum. I'm so sorry. About everything.' She reaches out to me; she puts her arm around my shoulders. 'It's OK, Mum,' she says. 'Everything's going to be all right.'

Maybe it is; there is no way of telling. But I sit here beside this young woman, my daughter, and feel a lightening of my burden. It is as if there is a new calmness radiating from Charlie, a calmness that imbues me almost with a sense of peace.

'Time to go,' I say at last. 'Time to move on. We've got a long drive ahead of us.'

We proceed in single file across the damp grass and past Jeff's grave. Charlie waits for me outside the porch of the church. I take her arm, and we walk down the gravel path. The lopsided tombstones seem to leer at us from each side, as if they are adjuring us to get on with living while we can. Framed by dark yew trees, the sky to the west glows briefly golden before the feeble sun vanishes and the evening quickens.

Charlie opens the lychgate and together we pass through. That hint of peace I began to feel earlier strengthens as, arm in arm, we stroll back to the car.

Acknowledgements

Thanks to Ali Arnold for her wise advice, Maggie Hamand for her friendship and instinct for what works and what doesn't, Kerrie Barnett for her many comments, Clare Christian, Heather Boisseau and Anna Burtt for getting this book into shape and out there. Mark Thompson for his advice on policing procedures, and Varuna the Writers' House for the opportunity to write with no interruptions when this was most needed.

Thanks also to my beloved family for listening to my obsessions — and my silences — while I wrote this book.

We do hope that you have enjoyed reading this large print book.

Did you know that all of our titles are available for purchase?

We publish a wide range of high quality large print books including:
Romances, Mysteries, Classics
General Fiction
Non Fiction and Westerns

Special interest titles available in large print are:
The Little Oxford Dictionary
Music Book
Song Book
Hymn Book
Service Book

Also available from us courtesy of Oxford University Press:
Young Readers' Dictionary
(large print edition)
Young Readers' Thesaurus
(large print edition)

For further information or a free brochure, please contact us at:
Ulverscroft Large Print Books Ltd.,
The Green, Bradgate Road, Anstey,
Leicester, LE7 7FU, England.
Tel: (00 44) 0116 236 4325
Fax: (00 44) 0116 234 0205

Other titles published by Ulverscroft:

THE FORRESTS

Emily Perkins

Dorothy Forrest is immersed in the sensory world around her; she lives in the flickering moment. From the age of seven, when her odd, disenfranchised family moves from New York City to the wide skies of Auckland, to the very end of her life, this is her great gift and possible misfortune. Through the wilderness of a commune, to falling in love, to early marriage and motherhood; from the glorious anguish of parenting to the loss of everything worked for and the unexpected return of love, Dorothy is swept along by time. Her family looms and recedes; revelations come to light; and death changes everything — but somehow life remains as potent as it ever was, and always has the potential to change 'if you're lucky enough to be around for it'.

THE TOWN

Shaun Prescott

A writer arrives in a dead-end town in the heart of the outback, rents a room, and begins a treatise on the disappearing towns of the Central West of New South Wales. But are the towns in decline — or are they literally vanishing? Present is a collection of characters, including community radio host Ciara, who receives dozens of unmarked cassette recordings every week and broadcasts them to a listenership of none; publican Jenny, who runs a hotel with no patrons; and ex-musician Tom, who drives an impractical bus that no one ever boards. In a place of innumerable petrol stations, labyrinthine cul-de-sac streets, and ubiquitous drive-thru franchises, where are these people likely to discover the truth about their collective past — and can they do so before the town completely disappears?

A LONG WAY FROM HOME

Peter Carey

Irene Bobs loves fast driving. Her husband is the best car salesman in rural south eastern Australia. Together with Willie, their lanky navigator, they embark upon the Redex Trial, a brutal race around the continent, over roads no car will ever quite survive. *A Long Way from Home* is Peter Carey's thrilling high-speed story that starts in one way, then takes you to another place altogether. Set in the 1950s in the embers of the British Empire, painting a picture of Queen and subject, black, white and those in between, *A Long Way from Home* illustrates how the possession of an ancient culture spirals through history — and the love made and hurt caused along the way.

SHELL

Kristina Olsson

Sydney, 1960s: Newspaper reporter Pearl Keogh has been relegated to the women's pages as punishment for her involvement in the anti-war movement, and is desperate to find her two young brothers before they are conscripted. Newly arrived from Sweden, Axel Lindquist is set to work as a sculptor on the Sydney Opera House. Haunted by his father's acts in the Second World War, he seeks solace in his attempts to create a unique piece that will do justice to the vision of Jorn Utzon, the controversial architect of the Opera House's construction. Pearl and Axel's lives orbit and collide, as they both struggle in the eye of the storm. This is a soaring, optimistic novel of art and culture, and of love and fate.